In the Hands of Death

The Eternal Heart Saga

Benjamin Anthony

authorHOUSE®

AuthorHouse™
1663 Liberty Drive
Bloomington, IN 47403
www.authorhouse.com
Phone: 1-800-839-8640

This is a work of fiction all characters, names, places and incidents are either the product of the author's imagination or used fictitiously any resemblance to actual events or locales or persons, living or dead, is entirely coincidental.

Published by AuthorHouse 10/27/2014

ISBN: 978-1-4685-5704-6 (sc)
ISBN: 978-1-4685-5705-3 (e)

Contents

Prologue...

Last January Eddy James case arrived at the judge's stand. Eddy was another john doe who had gotten in a mix up with notorious drug lords. They attempted to murder him and there had been a long battle in court. Unfortunately the public defender wasn't winning over the judge's confidence that day...

Court Room....

"Your Honor, in light of the brutal suffering of my client, Edward James, I asked that you to give him more medical attention and around the clock nursing." The public defender plead while standing at attention.

"Any comment, Counsel, in lieu the defense's statement?"

"I have no other comments as of right now, your Honor." The opposing counselor replied.

"Continue," returned the judge.

"Your Honor, Eddy James cannot survive in some state dungeon with substandard living conditions." The public defender announced while still searching for solace from the audience but shouts began to fill the room followed by the judges grim facial expression. Amid all of the negative re-verb from the audience, the public defender still managed to keep his ground against the nasty remarks from the audience.

"Order in the court!"

"Go on Counselor, will you?"

"How would you feel in my client's situation?" continued the public defender; Then he threw a stare of deep intention upon the jury, waiting to see if he found sympathy for the victim. Then the public defender ordered a courtroom monitor to be turned on. Eddy's appearance clinging to life support suddenly changed the mood of audience.

"Can't you see how my client is suffering?"

Guilt began to surface upon the faces of audience. It appeared the public defender couldn't seem to connect with the jury. Some grew weary of Eddy's suffering image and more remarks emerged again around the room. The monitor was turned off and the audience then became ravenous like wolves howling at the defense for the short visit with the live image. The public defender knew they craved to see more of Eddy's obscene misery.

"Jury, before you close your eyes on Eddy James's welfare, please consider his current plight of suffering," the public defender pleaded again. The public defender began to quickly realize defeat then slowly scampered back to his desk. The judge attention shifted from the monitor then, to his mighty gavel. Suddenly a loud clap from his hammer rang out and the raucous audience turned their attention back to the judge.

"Order!" The judge kept howling at the audience in an attempt to regain his custody over the kangaroo court.

"Knock-Knock!" The gavel was sent crashing repeatedly to the pulpit with menacing proportions. The noise began to subside and room became quiet again.

"Now we all know that the suffering of Eddy James is disheartening," the judge addressed the audience with vigor over the current matter and his face suddenly turned dourly as if he needed a drink.

"However, Eddy James's past criminal record has not shown this court that he was a good citizen," he persisted. "In fact, he was that to be so desired and there are just too many crimes that are stacked against him for such a request for more care in the state facility."

"But your honor," said the public defender.

"Sustained, Counselor!" The judge snapped back.

He began to cue the opposing counselor. The opposing counselor then immediately arose and stated his final argument.

"Clearly, your Honor, Eddy James, was into drugs, a suspect of murder in the late 90's, and teen gang violence," he continued. "The state has no obligation to help this social recluse any further!"

"May I object one more time, your Honor, in light of my client's current condition?" The public defender asked with a gentle outspokenness and then he threw steady glances between Eddy James's monitor and the vigilant audience.

"Permitted but this is your last statement." The judge replied.

"Your Honor, Edward James was left behind as a child in the back of an alley," rejection was still growing in number around the audience. "And later he had survived in the streets growing up as an adolescent."

"Get to the point!" The stern voice of the judge injected over the public defender's statement.

"Your Honor, there was no one there for Eddy as a youthful offender. Even God seemed to have forsaken him to be devoured by dark circumstances at an early age." The statement struck the judge's cold heart but the murky expressions written upon his face revealed that judgment on the matter was final.

"Your Honor, in closing I'd like to say, if there is any hope for Eddy James then let today be that day!" The public defender pronounced his last declaration of hope and waited patiently for the judge's word. The judge gave one last cold stare of condemnation that was cast upon the public defender. His morale weakened and his eyes dropped with regret. He felt there was nothing more to fight for.

"That would be all, your Honor." The public defender stated grimly.

"I can't let Mr. Edward James anywhere but the state sanitarium with the standard medical attention. I feel that he will have all of what the justice system can provide." Even the courtroom audience felt the cruel hands of death when the judge left Eddy' to worldly judgment.

"Adjourned!" Finally said the judge.

The life that was once Eddy James seemed to die with the last bang of the judge's weighty gavel. Court ended abruptly and no one was left behind except for a small framed Asian man wandering about aimlessly in the court room. He had been sulking in the shadows of the room for most of the day with confusion and sorrow. There had been some time that past since Eddy James had drove pedestrians around the city in one of his cabs for him. He even retired Eddy's cab for sentimental reasons and left his old dice on the rear view mirror.

Chapter 1: Lethal Injection

The night it all started,
September 29th, 10 O'clock P.M....

ANOTHER DARK OCCASION WAS BREWING at the corners of the city. The hoods were robbing, the hookers stalking and the pimps were dealing in indulgences. A deal was going down in Eddy James's old run-down apartment in Queens. He was a human statistic, drawn into the city's underworld by a fateful destiny. Godless in character, Eddy was a human with no sagacity for proper living. He was sure to maintain voluminous amounts of bad habits from marijuana to cocaine and if he lived past the next day without overdosing he was a lucky fool. His lose habits drew every scoundrel within the city who preyed upon him. One scoundrel who made profit out of the wickedness was known as, Angel Vasquez. He was a dark antagonist throughout Eddy's life. He made sure always kept to the shadows and only preyed on Eddy when he was craving for dope. Vasquez was well known to the underworld as an official mule for the drug lords and hazard to the local authorities. Vasquez was routinely perched over Eddy in his apartment.

"You want to get high tonight?" Asked Vasquez.

Eddy replied. “Right as always, Angel, but I only bought this sh*t from you last time ’cause it was the only drugs you had with you that night?” Eddy propped his fresh shaved head against a worn green sofa while preparing a spoon containing morphine. Aside from addiction Eddy was known for all his tattoos. He had white reptile-like skin with numerous amount of scars from fighting in gang wars. Eddy liked to reveal his diffident personality to others that passed him in the streets. Most of his scars and tattoos were obtained as a teenage gang member of the Dragons. The Dragons where known to rule the city papers with crime since the ‘80s, but Eddy never entertained them since he was a teen. Eddy’s friend, Mr. Li, found him an apartment close to work which wasn’t board-of-health worthy but it was all he could afford on a cabby’s salary. The efficiency had brown rugs stained and the walls were like that of a prison cell, pale and grease ridden.

“Where’s your girlfriend tonight?” Asked Angel. “What was her name again,” asked Vasquez smugly.

“You mean, Pandora?” Eddy returned.

“Yes, that’s her.” Angel was eluding to the lusty stripper, Pandora, whom Eddy had occasional sex with.

“She’s still pole-dancing back at the bar and doesn’t get off until morning.” Eddy remarked smartly. Vasquez eyes began to twitch as he patiently watched Eddy on the couch. Time seemed to be pressing on Vasquez’s consciousness. Finally, he sat down in an old easy-chair across from Eddy.

“Vasquez, throw me a spike will you?” Eddy thundered. He quickly pulled out a syringe from his leather jacket and handed it to Eddy.

“Hey,” replied Vasquez with attitude. “You know you still owed me two hundred from the last week.”

“You’ll get the money by the end of the night, ‘ESE.” Eddy barked then went back loading a syringe with dope.

"Damn, it's only midnight?" Vasquez thought to himself then glimpsed down at his shabby Rolex.

"Why so wired tonight?" Eddy asked with concern.

"I got to meet with Switchblade back at the bar." He continued shifting his eyes to a nearby window.

"How much is the syndicate getting out of this deal?" Asked Eddy. Vasquez began stroking his greasy-cropped curls.

"Nothing, not a dime tonight." He replied.

Suddenly Vasquez rose by the window and stood there impatiently. He began to run his hands across the pained glass and then decided to lift up on the window until it was opened. A nightly breeze flew into the room and he quickly noticed the alleyways were empty.

"Why are you by the window, Vasquez?" Remarked Eddy.

"You need some air in this room." He implied.

Although the moonlight revealed the trouble in Vasquez's eyes, Eddy, didn't sense anything wrong with him. Midst all his fears, Vasquez, felt the time was right to make profit with the new enticement. He strutted back towards the easy chair and sat down.

"How would you like something different, you know, to get high on?" Asked Vasquez. He began to search his coat pocket in a fit.

"What, like the heroin that you gave me the other tonight? It's not even dissolving." Cried Eddy.

"It's nothing you have ever done before." Vasquez spoke with devilish lips in an attempt to push the drug sale further. Eddy felt intrigued and tossed the heroin aside.

"Well what do you have?" Eddy asked with curiosity.

"The burn outs are calling red nine because when you get high you'll see red for nine hours." Vasquez explained.

"So, do you have it with you tonight?"

"Of course."

*"I need to try something new tonight." Eddy thought to himself. "The other sh*t he sold me has become obsolete. Besides Vasquez knew he owed me." He retrieved an oriental-styled box from his jacket then two vials were drawn out of the dragon etched wooden box.*

"This sh*ts like PCP but only better." Claimed Vasquez but Eddy still wore a look of doubt on his word.

"I'll take my chances on the bad heroin tonight." He replied smartly." Eddy picked up the spoon and began to light it up again. Vasquez grew irritated.

"This stuff was hard to find, 'ESE." Vasquez erupted off his chair.

"Easy, man, I'm just not interested tonight." Said Eddy to Vasquez.

The box fell to the floor amid the arguing and an antique syringe appeared among the scattered mess.

"What's the matter with you?" Vasquez continued. One of the drug vials on the floor seized Eddy and he came to wonder what was inside.

"Strange, where did you get these?" Eddy asked while picking up the drug vials.

"I bet you never saw dope carried like this before?" Vasquez tossed the crystal vials to Eddy. He noticed the tiny inscriptions but he couldn't decipher the ancient script. The fascination with the vessel began to compel Eddy to converge with the mysterious new drug.

"Tonight red-nine could be an interesting buzz?" Eddy thought while ogling the vial.

"I am only going to warn you once, the drug is lethal." Vasquez replied.

Chapter 2: The Deal

His hands now shuddered with excitement as the needle inched into his bulging vein. When the force of the alloy tip reached his body it gave him instant ecstasy. Eddy lost his equilibrium and dropped the drug needle. He strutted around the room feeling the new buzz.

"I never felt like this before." Eddy said with delight. The effect of the ancient sedative came swiftly with exhilaration. The drugs he used in the past often left him with emptiness but tsung-di seemed to fill his pallet that night. Although tsung-di was chilling ecstasy for Eddy and the poisonous effects began to linger within his body. A sharp pain emerged from his stomach.

"I don't feel so good?" Eddy replied.

Eddy's liver began to swell and his body was now riddled with toxicity. Finally his heart began to slow its beat. Writhing came with a violent force and the heaving wouldn't end. Vasquez noticed the trouble and rushed to console him.

"Go!"

Eddy began to scream in terror while twisted with pain. He spun about the room with madness was now swimming in his eyes. Vasquez disregarded the warning and Eddy charged at him in a fit of rage.

"Go!" Eddy snarled again.

Vasquez raced to the open window. Just as he began to feel free from his anxiety a set of tires screeched outside in the street. A black limousine appeared in front of the ghetto complex and a group of strange men stepped outside of the car. They began to circle the building with a large group. Clicking metal hammers echoed throughout the alleyway signaling that an immanent death was near. Vasquez held on to the black box tightly and started to creep closer toward the window's ledge.

He stopped moving around the room erratically and studied the faces of the triad moving from the third floor. Vasquez knew that they were only there for him. Eventually, they managed to barged into the main hall of the complex and stormed the flight of stairs like a team of bulls. Seconds later a loud crash came down upon Eddy's apartment door. Vasquez's heart was now racing with fear. Then another bang! came crashing down on the door. Finally Vasquez hurdled the open window for a quick get-away. He continued down the fire escape then vanished into the night. A dialect of Chinese resonated in discussions outside Eddy's apartment. He grew frightened and pressed his ear upon the door.

"Open up, we know you are in there!" A voice emerged.

"We came for what you took from us!" They continued. Eddy backed up from the door after the threats.

"Bang!" A large crash came on the door.

When the hinges were finally busted apart the triad flooded into the apartment.

"What are you doing here?" Eddy demanded with a drug induced slurred speech. Anger was planted upon the face of a thug standing next to Eddy.

"Where's the box?" Demanded the triad thug.

"What box?" Eddy cried.

The thug decided to make his final move.

"Bang!" A gunshot rang out.

The first blast shook the walls of the apartment and the force caught Eddy by surprise. The breach of the thugs .50 caliber was now steaming with hot metal and vengeance. Then suddenly a stream of bullets shattered through Eddy's bones until he reached the floor. He was paralyzed by the effects of the shots and his heart was giving into its last beats. The triads quickly fled the apartment and disappeared out of Eddy's life forever.

Chapter 3: Critical Condition

McCall's heart was racing with the anticipation of the previous gun play. He descended to the third floor with his 9 mm drawn. A man's remains we left swimming in gore.

"What a mess?" He thought trudging across the bloody carpet. The victims wrist was cold and limp he was too late.

Although he had seen worse homicides McCall still seemed to tremble at the sight of blood. Cash was strewn around the body and drenched in blood. He found a wallet next to the cash then rifled through it until he came across a license.

"What ever this fight was over," thought McCall. "It wasn't the money."

"Eddy James, born August '77. He's even an organ donor, not anymore?" A bout of sarcasm emerged from McCall's thoughts. "Druggies seemed to be dropping like flies around this section of the city."

He passed over the scene once more but no motives were clicking. The door was sprawled across the floor in large splinters. Different sized shoe prints were still imprinted all over the carpet but no one else was in sight. McCall felt a gang of men had to have busted in through the entrance with a great force and quickly left when they couldn't find what they were after.

"But why did they only kill this kid?" Thought McCall to himself.

A loud noise by a window sent McCall to his heels. He sprung to the open window and found a latter clanging against the brick wall. While motives kept spinning in McCall's mind he noticed the ballistic mortars that struck a nearby wall. He soon found a peculiar item glistening off the fire escape latter.

"Maybe they were after drugs?" He said while examining a vial containing a strange liquid substance.

Screaming began to amass down below. He pulled himself into the apartment and went back attending to the inspection of the crime. Suddenly a panting heavy-set man appeared by the entrance of the apartment. His round body leaned against the busted doorjamb.

"Holy, look at the f*ing mess in here!" He shouted while snapping his suspenders looser.

"Call 911, now!" McCall replied running out of breath.

"What happened to him?"

"Just go!" McCall returned.

Frank McCall was an undercover detective for the NYPD. He specialized in narcotics and this case was assigned to him three months ago after a suspect was taken into custody for dealing dope. The department later identified the suspect as, Angel Vasquez, residing in the vicinity of Queens at the time of his last arrest. The slime ball had been dealing drugs to the neighborhood kids before McCall received the case. Vasquez had a long list of assault charges and drug accounts. He had later found that Vasquez was also connected to one of the most sinister drug dealers in Chinatown.

Vasquez was just a small chink in the chain of ruthless drug dealers that sucked the tit of the local drug lords. But the department could not seem to get their hands on the "Opium King". Intelligence reports said the notorious Opium King had dealings with Vasquez on a regular basis. It was only a matter of time when the drug syndicate would fall and McCall was going to make sure it happened. Even though he was run ragged from chasing down crooks for twenty-two years he was the type of guy that would never let the system down. Finally paramedics flooded into the room. McCall was waiting outside of Eddy's apartment tapping his feet nervously. He began smoking a cigarette to kill his nervousness. Just as he felt relaxed a female EMT drenched in blood suddenly approached him.

"How long has the victim been in this condition?"

McCall replied. "About a half an hour."

"What's going on?" He demanded. The medic didn't answer but instead she remained tying the bloody body to the stretcher.

The medic quickly radioed. "We have a victim of a shooting still alive!" An obscure cry resonated from under the sheets. McCall reclined in fear as the covered body limped around on the stretcher.

"He's still alive, impossible?"

Chapter 4: Dick Davis

The next day...

The precinct was humming its usual chatter of typewriters, the slam of file drawers and useless chitchat. McCall remained at his desk review the facts of the new shooting.

"What was Eddy doing the night before? Who was he with?" He began to jot the questions down in a fresh report. The shadow of a short man suddenly overwhelmed his desk.

"You're in my light." The bulky image seemed to cover McCall like nightfall. Dick Davis was waiting impatiently for the new report. Davis appeared to be a stocky, African-American who was known around the precinct to have a mean temperament and a hard nose for gruesome homicides. Davis was still sweating over the heat from the media after the last homicide.

"McCall," he thundered.

"What do you have so far on last night's shooting?"

"Oh, captain, I am still working on the case." Replied McCall acting as if Davis wasn't there.

"Do you even have a thing finished," he continued. "It seems to me that you like to take your good old time with reports, McCall, is that true?" Davis kept implying back to McCall. He returned with a wry look then dove right back into typing.

"I've been working on this damn report all night, Captain Davis, you got to give me a break." McCall returned. The captain scoffed at his diligence and began to page through a file.

"Did you know the last homicide we investigated is now plastered all over the nightly news? The public now thinks that this department has dropped the ball and I am the only one that feels the heat!" Davis seemed to quiver at his own words well knowing that thirty-five years of police work still wasn't enough to keep the criminals behind bars.

"Look, I am doing the best I can right now." McCall said then shoved a file folder at Davis.

"Well, what can you tell me now?" Davis begged with patience glued around his eyes.

"I know the victim is still alive at St. Vincent's intensive care." McCall answered back but Davis just appeared doubtful.

"The medical report said they found enough bullets in the chump to put a water buffalo down and he is still alive?" Davis said raving with suspicion over the medical reports.

"All I have as of right now, captain, is that a drug pusher may have shot the victim. The suspect may be Angel Vasquez," McCall continued. The facts weren't settling with the captain's reservations anymore. He leaned his muscular forearms on a pile of old case files and continued to read the police briefing.

"You mean the bum that we hauled in here last month?" Asked Davis.

"I still can't finger exactly how many shooters there were that night?" He replied shuffling ballistic documents with nervy fingers.

"Well, it's not like the old days, McCall," Davis said with sincerity.

"When you find one crook you've found them all." The captain placed the report carefully back on his desk and stood proudly before McCall.

"What do you think is going wrong?" McCall asked.

"In today's world many complications arrive in these homicides. One king-pin runs this whole part of town and he's got everybody pinned as his mule to boot. This city has become a nightmare I tell you." Cried Davis.

"The Opium King assignment is coming to you soon," he continued. "Detective Smith and Neumann is wrapping up the final investigation as we speak and I volunteered you to do a follow up investigation."

"Thanks, captain."

Davis turned away from McCall's desk and disappeared into the crowded city precinct hall. Nothing seemed to matter now to McCall but the final investigation of the Opium King and Eddy's mysterious shooting. There still remained too many unanswered questions. For now McCall was on his own if he wanted to find out more on the Eddy James case.

St. Vincent's Hospital....

Later on that week McCall visited St. Vincent's located a few blocks from the precinct. Other than some shoddy brick work & cement, prayers, seemed to be the only thing holding up the facade of the old city hospital. Nurses and doctors were spread about the hallways while attending to patients. McCall reached the intensive care unit on the second floor. He slithered around the crowd shaking the cold off of his issued fog jacket.

"You look like you could use some coffee?" McCall opened conversation to a young nurse snapping gum. He studied her carefully. The nurse's attention was immediately cast upon McCall. When she examined his figure her eyes sparked with desire for McCall's rugged good-looks. She shifted her attention from paper work and fixed some loose hair behind her ear before she talked to him.

"Tell me about it?" She finally replied.

"You look really busy tonight." McCall remarked while the nurse fumbled around with more medical documents.

"They took over a dozen overdoses just last night." She said.

"That had to be a record?" McCall joked but she was run ragged from the late night to laugh back. She simply smirked at him and dove back into her work.

"Who were you here to see again?" She inquired while paging through a document. McCall could tell she rarely trusted anyone from the coldness in her stares. He shifted his weight around then dug into his pockets and pulled out some municipal paper work.

"I'm here for a man that survived a shooting last night." He replied. McCall handed her an official document. She skimmed then passed it back to McCall.

"Detective Frank McCall where's your badge?" She returned sarcastically.

"I don't always were my badge around the city it's bad for my stealthy image." He returned smartly.

"May be you should wear it more often, you kind of gave me a little scare." She continued.

"Naturally." He replied.

"So, is this official police work or just visiting?" She asked.

"For now just visiting." McCall replied.

"We normally don't let non-relatives in intensive care at this hour unless its an emergency."

"I'll have to come by another day." He said and began to walk away from her station.

"Wait," She exclaimed. McCall turned to face her.

"I'm listening?" He replied.

"I'll let you pass this time. His room is the third door on the right. You can't miss it." She winked and pointed toward the hallway.

"Thank you, miss." He said then scurried away.

McCall had no idea what to expect when he met with Eddy after the tragic shooting. Not to mention the department still couldn't get over the fact that Eddy James had survived. McCall found the room and stood by the entrance. He noticed Eddy James sitting upright on the hospital bed busy reading a sports magazine.

"It says here," he said aloud. "That New York's all-star pitcher, Keith Knight, might get traded next season to Chicago." Eddy's stony voice shook the silence of the room. McCall reclined with alarm. Eddy had been weeks in a coma and yet no one that he knew cared enough to visit until McCall showed up. McCall looked familiar to Eddy but he couldn't explain who he was. Aside from the head trauma he had recollections of his past but some memories still lingered with uncertainty. Then Eddy felt like he pinned McCall's character into his memory.

"That's a bummer for New York they'll be missing his famous curve ball." McCall replied trying to get acquainted with Eddy. He remained quiet for just a moment then decided to rise off the bed.

"They said I would've never made it alive if I had not been saved seconds after the shots were fired." Eddy replied. Eddy threw the magazine on the bed and tore off his hospital gown and exposed his scarred appearance. The wounds covered the surface of his body. Stitches were strewn across his head and face. Most of the wounds were stained with blood and covered with gauze. His cheekbones were sunken and his skin pale. Eddy appeared to McCall as though he were the walking dead. The freakish image gripped McCall then Eddy finally placed his gown back over his body.

"Say, don't you live on the floor above me?" Eddy answered as he fixed McCall into his psyche.

"I moved there a few months ago."

"I knew your face looked familiar. So you're the cop that lives above me?" Eddy said.

"I am not the same guy I assure you." McCall returned.

"I know everybody who goes in and out of that building!" Eddy proclaimed with twitch in his eye. McCall began to turn nervously in his chair.

"Damn, he recognized me." McCall said to himself.

"You must be a.." Eddy snapped.

"What if I was just a concerned neighbor who came to the hospital of my free time?" McCall persisted.

"You're the guy that used to visit a patrol car in the alley every night at six o'clock sharp." Eddy hissed with anger.

"What you want from me?" McCall fired back.

"I want you to leave!" Eddy demanded then he pointed to the door. McCall quickly rose from his chair and appeared to Eddy as if he was going to answer.

"Fine." McCall replied then left the room.

Chapter 5: Six O'clock

The next day dusk finally settled over the city's skyline as McCall entered the precinct and sat down at his desk. He picked up the final briefing of the Opium King and began to read down the document. He reviewed the report and the same nick-name appeared "*Switchblade*". Switchblade was described in the report also known as one Mickey the "Blade" Danozzio. He was a killer as well as a low-level middleman for the Opium King. The system let Switchblade go as a last minute bait and switch operation but McCall knew it was time to reel him in. Drug enforcement listed him having many connections to the underground with insurmountable drug arrests. In a statement to investigators while under custody for drug trafficking he had reported on location of facilities owned by the Opium King.

Switchblade was a key character in the whole drug ring however his loyalties to the police or the Opium King were to be so desired. McCall read down the fourth page of the report which detailed that Switchblade ran a drug lab located under a strip bar in Chinatown. A seedy place known as The Purple Lady. The briefing also reported that they were producing meth, cocaine and opium under the Opium King's constituents. Smith and Neumann had the place under surveillance for several months and McCall was to finished the job. A covert swat was able to pinpoint the building exits but the underground rooms were still undiscovered locations. McCall knew that it was where Switchblade did most of his own hustling.

The Purple Lady...

McCall had entered the club hoping to nab Switchblade quickly but he only found a over crowed bar filled with inequity. Switchblade was described in the briefing as a taller man with a bald head and one eye made of blue glass. He had a thin go-tee and was forced to use a cane after a recent incident with the police. McCall was abhorred by the mirage of cigarette smoke emanating throughout the bar while he scanned among the crowded the place for Switchblade. Finally after the last stripper left the main stage he spotted Switchblade talking to a leggy red-head bearing her breasts. McCall pushed through the crowd of noisy people and pulled up a stool next to Switchblade. He was dressed finely with black leather pants and a blue dress shirt neatly tucked. Switchblade took a careful look at McCall standing close to him. Then he turned back to the bar tender.

"Hey, Tommy, bourbon!" Belted Switchblade across bar.

The bar tender was quick with Switchblade's drink. A topless stripper dazzled in sequence strutted across the granite bar top in front Switchblade. He began to wave money before the naked dancer.

"Take a look at the set on that!" Switchblade shouted aloud and then threw five hundred buck at her like nothing. He turned to McCall again and pointed to her naked chest. The stripper flung the rest of her sequence outfit across the bar and McCall finally smiled proudly at the advice.

"Hey, the old lady doesn't put-out anymore?" McCall asked teasing Switchblade over the five hundred bucks.

"Can't you see I'm single," he continued. "No married man drops five hundred on a set like that besides if my old lady ever turned me down I'd tell her to go fist herself." He belted out proudly. McCall slowly rose, put his arm around Switchblade's shoulder and then he whispered carefully into his ear.

"Where have you been, Mickey, the boy's down at the precinct are getting a little edgy."

"What do mean by that?"

"You haven't been visiting us very anymore." Switchblade became disoriented upon McCall's inquiry and froze in place.

"How did we meet again and how do you know my name?" Switchblade replied.

McCall suddenly grabbed Switchblade arm then escorted him out of the noisy crowd.

"Easy, man, I still don't know you." Switchblade cried drunkenly.

"Shut up and come with me!" McCall commanded while he pressed Switchblade closer to the restrooms.

"Hey, man, if you wanted to get physical tonight I'm sure one of the bar queens can help you out." Switchblade said trying to buck out of McCall's grip. He barged through the bathroom doors. McCall remained poised over Switchblade and pinned him to the wall.

"You don't leave here until you show me what's under this bar." Growled McCall.

"Alright, baby!" Said Switchblade with drunken slur the threat seem to put fear at his heels.

"Whatever it is we can work this thing out." Switchblade backed himself into a small corner and he pulled a hidden blade from under his sleeve.

"So, where's the drug lab, Mickey?" McCall demanded.

Switchblade played a dead hand until vengeance got the best of him and he took a swing at the detective. McCall dodged the blade and seized him by the wrist and threw Switchblade down onto the bathroom floor.

"Where is the lab?" Replied McCall. Switchblade grew an ill-faded smile. McCall suspicions said that he was hiding more than just the drug lab.

"Tell me now." McCall fired.

"You'll get nothing out of me." Switchblade returned with venom this time. McCall's grip got tighter around Switchblades throat.

"I'm not much of a negotiator but I know for a fact that they are always making more room for the next pole queen of-the-month back in the slammer," McCall warned. "Now, tell me how I can access the drug lab and maybe I'll cut you a deal."

"Okay, on the other side of that bathroom stall there's a sliding pocket door along the wall. Push it aside and walk into the small room. When you're past the door there's an electric main switch push it down and a cover in the floor will slide back. Go down the hole in the floor and follow the corridor underground. The warehouse is there." McCall pulled out some handcuffs and began to read him his Miranda rights.

"You have the right to remain silent until I get back. So get acquainted with the sh*t-fountain until my team comes for you." He flipped around the out of order sign hanging outside the bathroom door and found the pocket door then entered the small room beyond it. McCall felt around for the switch. He quickly found the main and methodically turned on the switch. The ground shook beneath him and a hidden cover slid back in the floor and then he climbed down the latter with caution. McCall slowly walked down the narrow hallway. The hallway was dark and only a few dim bulbs glimmered overhead and came upon a pair of steel doors with a peephole.

McCall glanced into the peephole. The lab was empty so he pushed through the doors. Among the lab vials and scales he noticed more unopened bags of toxic substance and apparatuses for illicit drugs. He also found a crates of refined opium that were being prepared for shipment. McCall picked up the sample of fluid contained in the steel pails and took a sample of the fluid. There was a desk at the corner of the opium lab. He found more documents exposing their daily shipments. After McCall confiscated the information he took a few camera shots of the lab. All this fresh information would surely collapse the Opium King. The sound of the automatic doors echoed into the hallway and it resonated into the lab.

"Someone is coming. I better find some cover." Thought McCall.

Just then two over-sized men came into the lab from the hallway.

"Did you see what he did to Switchblade?" The sound of the henchmen made McCall's heart race with fear.

"He's got to be around here just look?" One shouted.

"They found out my handy work back in the bathroom stall," McCall thought to himself.

He kept searching and soon noticed another way out of the lab. A glass block wall appeared and McCall found a doorway connected to alleyway. A closet door near by was notably the only way to the room behind the glass wall. He passed bye a few feet from the desk and finally entered the closet. McCall heard men scuffle around the lab looking for something.

"I think he's down here." One of the guards shouted.

Although there was little evidence of McCall's presence they found the main doors slightly ajar. He studied them carefully to get a better look at their position. He noticed two large thugs searching the lab armed with sub-machine guns. McCall still remained calm over the stormy situation while he came up with another plan of escape. He opened the closet doors slightly and scanned the lab. McCall knew that chances for survival were slimming down. He shut the closet door carefully then attempted to search for any more hidden doors along the back wall. Among a collection of brooms there were only bags of trash and rodents in the closet along with the detective. McCall began to study the sewer rats passing freely between concrete walls and the outside alleyway and he felt a some air coming through the cracks in the wall. He began to remove the brooms and kicking rodents away from the trash. McCall checked the walls for a hollow spot with his hands. Basement door appeared which were a part of the alleyway. The sound of footsteps suddenly alarmed McCall. He searched for the buried door handle lever and quickly slid his hand across the hidden metal door. A refuge where the club dumped nightly trash appeared and he tore through piled garbage bags until a ladder appeared. The ladder led into the back alley. McCall quickly exited the trash bunker through the double doors. A small swat unit was parked a block away from the bar waiting for the detective.

Chapter 6: The Dragon's Eye

McCall settled in his chair and started to review the last nights clues. The journal noted when shipments of opium came in on the east & west coast as well as distribution of the smuggled drug. The drop areas included surrounding northern and southern regions of the city. These key locations would help the system to cut the drug ring off at the pass and a new sting was put into effect. The shipments from foreign shores would have to be taken over by the feds but McCall's district's main concern was the opium that came into the city. McCall discovered the shipments were being delivered under the name of an unknown pharmaceutical company known as, "Three Oceans Pharmaceutical, they were selling the liquid form to area hospitals as morphine. The cover gave the Opium King a good camouflage in avoiding international authorities. The sample of liquid that he previously attained in the drug lab contained refined opium that was used for the production of liquid heroin.

The new information gave McCall a good idea on what the cartel's were selling illegally to the street junkies. It was getting late at the precinct and McCall felt it was time to wrap up. McCall put the final touches on the report before he placed it on the captain's desk. Just as everything was cleared he remembered the vial he found at Eddy's apartment the other night. McCall placed it in his palm and viewed it closely.

"This was no ordinary vessel." Thought McCall.

He found that the casing had a dragon's eye engraved upon it along with strange script writings. The drug inside had a distinct resemblance to the chemical structure of opium and it was not the run-of-the-mill street drug. The facts were piling up after hours and McCall decided to hang it up. He soon left the precinct and left his work for tomorrow.

McCall's apartment...

He hung up the car key's after the late night sting at the station. A cool breeze from and open window sent him a sudden chill. He drew his gun and began searching the apartment. The rooms turned up empty. After all was clear in the room he felt it was okay to rest his gun on the kitchen table. The fridge door was slightly open and he found a blade and note was found dug into the table. McCall picked the knife out of its place. The note read, *"I got your number!"* Suddenly a cold steel revolver was pressed subtlety against his face. The silhouette of Switchblade appeared grinning out of the darkness of the room.

"Switchblade?" Replied McCall.

"Where's my shipment journal?" Said Switchblade moving closer to McCall.

"I don't have a clue?" McCall snapped.

"Better find one!" Replied Switchblade then he readily cocked the hammer of his revolver and held his aim upon McCall. He remained frozen in place. Switchblade gripped McCall and placed him into submission. He began to press his fingers into a pressure point under McCall's neck.

"Don't mess with me!" Switchblade growled. McCall gripped the handle of a hidden derringer under his the sleeve of his shirt but waited for the right moment to strike.

"The gig is up, Switchblade, even if you do kill me you won't get far the government already has all the info on the lab." Switchblade's hardness lighten up at the cheap threat.

"Who has whose number now!" Returned McCall. Switchblade finally loosen his grip on McCall's throat. McCall felt free and decided to strike when Switchblade wasn't looking.

"Crack!"

McCall struck Switchblade with the butt end of his hand. He pointed the derringer at Switchblades face then snatched his gun from the nearby table.

"Say, didn't I flush you down the toilet?" McCall remarked proudly while placing freeze on Switchblade's forehead.

"I managed to climb out!" Switchblade answered.

Switchblade suddenly got lose from McCall's aim. He manage to kick the gun from McCall's grip and finished with a sucker punch to his gut.

"Let's go back to the station!" Switchblade growled while pointing his gun back at McCall.

"What makes you think I am taking you anywhere?" McCall replied.

"Your girlfriend," Switchblade wielded a picture of a girl he stole from McCall's kitchen.

"Checkmate!" McCall thought to himself wishing that he had shot Switchblade earlier.

"She found a comfy spot in the back seat of my car." Replied Switchblade keeping a stone-faced look upon McCall.

"What did you do to Taylor you scum?" McCall answered.

"I did nothing to her yet," he returned. "I just took her for a little ride to find you." McCall was shoved into his car with a gun still tagged to his back. Taylor was bound and gagged in the back seat of a '66 Lincoln. McCall slowly took the tape off of her mouth and ran his hand through her long black hair.

"Taylor, are you okay?" McCall asked with sincerity in his eyes.

"Bastard doesn't know how to treat a lady. You should keep your fried here on a leash!" She replied while kicking the back of his seat.

"What did you expect Don Juan saving you?" He chuckled.

"He's no friend." Replied McCall.

The car ride back to the precinct wasn't long and Switchblade found a safe spot next to the building.

"Make it fast!" Switchblade barked at McCall.

He raced down the hall way and busted into the main office. He tore through his notes and found the journal. It wasn't long before it was back in Switchblade's hands again.

"We'll She continued. then sped off leaving them to find their own way home.

Chapter 7: Eddy's Unexpected Recovery

Meanwhile across the city...

THE MOON OVER NIGHT SKY was like an giant spotlight beaming over a hospital building and Eddy had been laid up in his room for three weeks now. A doctor suddenly entered his room. Eddy James was still coping with his new ability. He knew why he did not die from gun shot wounds but the medical team at St. Vincent's still couldn't figure out the phenomenon.

"Hello, Mr. Eddy James?" The doctor replied. Eddy sat up at attention. He began fixed his medical gown in a nervous fit.

"Now open your mouth for me." The doctor asked then forced a tongue depressor down Eddy's esophagus.

"Okay, Eddy, you can lie down now." The doctor replied.

"What's the diagnosis?" Eddy returned while lying down on a cot.

"This is just a routine inspection before the hospital will release you."

"Disrobe, please." Eddy quickly dropped his gown and the doctor began to study Eddy's wounds.

"Interesting?" Replied the doctor gently dropping his monocles.

"You've healed nicely no thanks to your government health plan, eh?" Teased the doctor.

"Sometimes I think I am better off dead." Eddy returned.

"I am afraid some of our lab rats found a strange narcotic in your blood stream." The doctor was enthusiastic over the new medical case and his stare grew intently upon Eddy James.

"What do you mean?" Eddy's face suddenly filled with alarm over the doctor's report.

"Let's be honest with each other tonight, Eddy, what other drug do you take socially?"

He began to hesitate for a moment before the doctors inquiry.

"Mostly heroine." He replied while the doctor shined a light into his pupils.

"I feel it's in your best interest to see our staff psychologists before leaving." The doctor replied in hopes that he would find a reason to go the therapy and change.

"I know I'm addict. I don't need someone else to tell me!" He replied.

"Then we may have enforce the law, your choice?" The doctor explained coldly.

"So, you're going to sick the boys-in-blue on me, eh?" Eddy protested then shook his head with doubt.

"I'm afraid so." He answered.

The doctor brushed Eddy off quickly then disappeared out of the room. Eddy finally fled the hospital after meeting the shrink and signing paper work. He was free again to embrace the dark city streets. He traveled down the desolate street alone and past memory surfaced of the tragic night. The mysterious whereabouts of Vasquez also began to weigh on this mind. Vengeance was a thought that kept filling his mind every time he thought of Vasquez. Eddy kept searching around the city corners to satisfy his revenge but Vasquez was not among the nighttime druggies. The nightly search grew weary but the facade of The Purple Lady suddenly appeared. Eddy knew it as a place where many rogues hung their hat. He entered the smoky bar hoping find some live entertainment. His eyes pierced through the stuffy room filled with dancing sluts and drunken winos. He carefully scanned every corner of the bar looking for Vasquez but he wasn't showing up in the crowd.

"He's must be here with Switchblade?" Eddy thought to himself.

Pandora, the local favorite showgirl, was now dancing topless in Eddy's sights. The regular's called her *Pandora* because her sultry dances seemed to lure everyone. Eddy studied her closely as Pandora's shapely hips danced between the shadows and the radiance of the spotlight. Her nakedness began to occupy his lonely thoughts and his worries seem to disappear for the night.

"Tommy, how have you been?" Eddy shouted while poking through the large crowd of drunks until he reached the counter.

"I've been busier than a ghetto bust stop." The bar tender returned sarcastically Eddy always cracked a smile at his wit.

"So?" He replied with his beady eyes fixed upon the bartender.

"Where's Switchblade been these days, Tommy?" Eddy shouted over the loud music.

"There was another mix up with the cops," he answered. "They almost shut this place down again."

"No kidding?" Eddy clamored.

"Switchblade around tonight?" Cried Eddy. "I got to get another fix for the night."

"I don't know, Eddy?" Tommy snapped back at him.

"Get me a shot of liquor, will you?" Replied Eddy.

"I can't afford any wild behavior tonight," Tommy warned. "I'll have to throw your ass out with the trash!"

"Get me that drink and we'll have no problems." He growled back at the bartender then snatched some pills from his coat. He popped a few and stumbled over to the center stage where Pandora was wrapping up her last topless dance.

Chapter 8: Pandora

Pandora was drawn to *white trash* ever since her queer uncle John *made her* in the back of a beat-up '55 caddy. She was only twelve. Eddy's seedy appearance seemed to stimulate that strange mechanism in her sexual desires and she was drawn to him at first glance. After a few drinks and a few cheap pickup lines Eddy escorted her back to his new apartment for the night. He began to put hands through her long blonde hair and she grasped onto his torso tighter. Since Pandora was free and Eddy was lonely the interlude came about for the right reasons. Before she could peel off her garments they were re-living the second-rate passion on his worn-out waterbed. Eddy knew the danger of sleeping with such a chick like Pandora but neither one of them seemed to care that night. There was no guilt between them but Eddy knew he would have to account for sleeping with Pandora later.

Next day...

The morning broke and Pandora had been gone for a while. Eddy began the day on a quest to find the whereabouts of Vasquez. He wanted some answers about the shooting from weeks ago but Vasquez was not showing up at the local drug corners of Chinatown and time was getting stale. Eddy found himself back at the new apartment again. He found the couch and fell fast asleep. Midnight then came quickly and there was a knock at the door. He jumped up and dug for the revolver from under his pillow.

"Who is there?" Shouted Eddy in apprehension. He waited patiently at the door.

"It's Vasquez," the voice replied. "Open up!" Eddy unlocked the door, released the hammer of his revolver and let Vasquez inside.

"You're alive?" Vasquez asked gazing upon Eddy with looks of surprise.

"What do you care?" Eddy snapped then turned away from Vasquez. He could feel the weight of Eddy's anger but it didn't seemed to bother him.

"How did you get this address?" Replied Eddy.

"I got it from the superintendent back in Queens. It took a long time getting here with all the expressway traffic." Vasquez said then limped into the apartment while holding of his injured arm.

"What happened to you?" Eddy inquired then closed the door behind Vasquez.

"You weren't the only one that took a few bullets the night of the shooting." Vasquez remarked then sat back in the easy chair.

"You left me to die!" Eddy erupted.

Vasquez kept calm when Eddy had the outburst. He rose and began to paced the floors of the apartment.

"You knew those guys didn't you?" Eddy cried.

"You should have died that night, Eddy" Remarked Vasquez.

"I'm sorry that I left but there were other problems going on with me that night." Eddy began to light up a cigarette.

"I want to know who they where?" Eddy begged.

"They were triads." Said Vasquez to Eddy.

"Triads?" Eddy replied surprised.

"They were here for me." He said.

"Why did they shoot me then?" Said Eddy with disbelief.

"I don't know, they were crazy."

"No, really, why?"

"They were after the drug I stole from them." Vasquez finally answered.

"This is not good, Vasquez, the Fists I could deal with but not triads!" Eddy began to grow nervous.

"Don't worry they think I'm on the other side of town tonight." Replied Vasquez.

"What are we supposed to do if they find us again?" Eddy said.

"I don't know but you need to lie low for a while." Vasquez said grimly. Even though Eddy and Angel may have been at odds, he never let Vasquez down. They shared a past life that most friends would not have survive if they were not together; a life of pain and survival. They would never forget that they were Dragons.

Chapter 9: The Survivor

The next night...

EDDY TOOK UP HIS SHIFT and rode down the city streets searching for desperate pedestrians. After a few hours of driving he found two men shivering out in the cold November air. Eddy stopped by the curb and let two foreign men in the cab.

"Thanks, pal, the cold was really getting to us!" The pedestrian moaned in broken English then slammed the cab door shut.

"Where to?" asked Eddy.

"Some where we could get some entertainment, you know, what I mean!" Exclaimed the foreigner in code.

"I know a perfect place." Said Eddy He put the cab into drive and pressed down on the accelerator. He continued down the main street until he came upon "The Purple Lady". They piled out of the cab and paid the cab fair. It was the end of Eddy's shift and he decided it was time to nod off for a while. He pulled into the back alley and drifted off to sleep. A few minutes passed and Switchblade appeared in Eddy's rear view mirror, He came storming out of the bar.

"Get out of the car!" Switchblade snapped at Eddy hanging his head half outside the open cab window.

"What's gotten into you?" Eddy asked still disillusioned from lack of sleep. "This isn't about Pandora?" Eddy hopped out of the cab with clenched fists.

"You got to pay tonight!" Switchblade kept repeating.

"If this is over Pandora you already lost this one." Eddy replied with a grim stare aimed upon Switchblade.

"People are telling me that you were with Pandora the other night?" Switchblade thundered at Eddy.

"I didn't think you cared about her that much?" Eddy returned arrogantly.

"She's mine, dead beat, stay away for her!" Switchblade remarked with ferocity.

"Are you sure she is just yours it appears to me the whole bar has her almost every night?" Eddy replied smartly.

"I am the one who scraped her off the goddamn streets and gave her a life!"

"She's just a homeless smut to you!" Eddy roared back at him. Switchblade suddenly swarmed him like angry bees with punches. Eddy went sprawling to the pavement.

"How many times did you f* her last night?" Switchblade cried swinging his fists around in the air. Eddy jumped to his heels prepared to fight Switchblade.

"I did her so many times she needed a walker to get home!" Eddy joked smartly but Switchblade wasn't. He slyly pulled out his blade and waved it around threateningly. In the distance two bouncers appeared before Eddy and Switchblade watching as the fight drew on.

"Bruno, Ray, make a saint out of this loser!" Commanded Switchblade. The muscle-heads swarmed Eddy with punches and he nearly collapsed. He even returned some blows but they only angered the huge behemoths. The violence kept coming upon him and Eddy could no longer duck the punches and he began to stumble from the blows. When Eddy could no longer stand the bouncers threw him into the street.

"I never want to see you around here again especially around Pandora." Switchblade belted.

Eddy returned to his apartment in tatters and dropped to his knees in misery. He felt coldness creeping into his veins again and began to enter a trance of confusion over the night. Eddy knew that Switchblade was going to be back. He limped into the kitchen and fixed some ice for his ribs. The broken bones were unbearable and breathing became a chore. Eddy began to check out his wounds in front of the hall mirror.

"I should get to a hospital." He felt under the couch for an old stash of heroine. He quickly doped up the needle and the shot sent some of the pain away. Eddy knew his life was in jeopardy now that Switchblade knew of this affairs with Pandora. Then the phone suddenly rang and Eddy answered.

"Why aren't you on your shift yet?" Mr. Li asked in anger over the phone line.

"I got caught in a traffic before I reached the interstate." Eddy replied slyly to his boss.

"Don't forget the wages come out of your pay check!" Threatened Li. Eddy slammed down the receiver.

Chapter 10: McCall's Interlude

Back at McCall's office...

THE SECOND REPORT ON THE vial was placed on McCall's desk. The translation finally had been sent down by forensics lab. He opened the file folder and reviewed the data. One of the article publicized mentioned the name of an ancient man was the main character in the article. He was a character of royal influence that lived during the oppression of the Zhou dynasties. His name was revealed to McCall as Chao Huang. He once discovered a plant, tsung-di, which no longer exists in Asia. The plant was once grown wild in the areas of Shaanxi province and Chao discovered medicinal uses during the agriculture movement in Chinese history. McCall began to read further down the article from the daily news.

"Daily City News"..

> *"Artifact Theft"*
> *Nu Shangxi claimed that her family had been producing wares and vessels since early China. With the help of*

> *archaeologist's, Shangxi, recently discovered an ancient town in the Chinese mountain regions, where the Huang's ancestors may have once lived. The geographic location of the Shaanxi providence was an upper plateau region of China. A small village once thrived there. The dig site revealed bits of ceramic and porcelain wares that may have been traded to different parts of the east. Also found near the site were ancient timber ships. The archaeologist's followed the clues of the expedition and found the wreckage of a timber ship off the coast of the China Sea, including a peculiar sealed ebony box.*

Nu began the excavation of a historic man named Chao Huang ten years ago. And she discovered that Huang was a medicine man in the village of Shaanaxi and the container that was unearthed may have held the key to a ancient sedative, tsung-di, meaning that was relevant to *Xian* or to give one immortality. Chao ancient clue came into McCall's reality but he still needed to find out more. He read the top headline of the news article Nu Shangxi was top priority to interview. He finally pinned down Nu Shangxi after a few phone calls and set to meet with her later on that week.

Nu Shangxi's office...

Later on that day McCall met with Nu Shangxi at her Yangtze Shipping. He arrived at the main hallway of the warehouse building and checked in with security. The guard kindly escorted him up stairs to Nu Shangxi's main office. The office was decorated with oriental motifs that she obtained mostly from the dig site. There were hand-crocheted tapestries neatly hung on the four walls of her office. Among the other furnishings there were two end-tables both made of stained timber wood from the Zhou dynasty inlaid with granite. McCall noticed a screen art painting from medieval China.

"You have a copy of the Eight Immortals, Ming Dynasty?" McCall recited. Nu instantly became impressed with him.

"It's the original copy, if you needed to know, detective. You really have and eye for Chinese artists." She replied.

Nu was a shrewd businesswoman as well as an avid art collector. Aside from falling for Nu's riches, most men fell for her soft eyes and a youthful complexion but McCall kept the visit just business. Although she was nearly fifty her athletic figure seemed to keep her looking twenty years younger.

"It's a shame that I have so little time to enjoy my collection." She replied.

"Ring!" The phone sounded in the office.

"Excuse me, for a moment, I have to take this new call.

"Hello?" Nu jumped in anticipation for the call.

Nu spoke quickly over the phone then readily hung up the receiver.

"I'm sorry, Detective McCall, let us start over again." She said.

"Sit down why don't you?" She replied.

McCall finally sat down on a dated plush Dynastic chair.

"How do you do?" She greeted him earnestly while hanging up the phone.

"Good, Miss Shangxi," he replied. "I came here of course to talk to you about the vial I found while I was on duty."

"May I see it?" She asked. He rose and handed the vial to Nu. She carefully viewed the image of a dragon's eye on the vial.

"Ah, this was the capsule which is a part of a container that was unearthed out of the South China Sea," she explained. "My archaeologist stopped digging just a few years ago."

"I read the past articles you are a very interesting antiquarian, Miss Shangxi." McCall replied.

"Well, as you know we lost the container only few months ago after the break in and we've been trying to locate it ever since." She continued. "The container alone is worth millions and we would like to have it back in our possession."

"Where did you find this?" She probed while waiting patiently for his answer.

"I found the vial in an apartment building in Jackson Heights." McCall replied. "And it just so happened that it was during the time of a shooting." McCall's suspicions began to solidify when Nu reclined at the news.

"Interesting?" Nu replied then placed a curious stare back upon McCall. She then picked up the receiver to her phone and began to dial out.

"Would you know anything about the past shooting, Miss Shangxi?"

"Why, no, detective, will you excuse me, I must use the phone again." She said.

McCall suddenly grew nervous about Nu Shangxi character. New questions began spinning in his mind about Nu Shangxi but no answers were matching. Nu appeared to be clean but McCall smelled trouble with her export business. She talked quietly into the receiver routinely using native dialect. Nu finally hung up the phone and focused her attention back upon McCall. Nu held her frame firmly before the detective even though she felt his suspicions.

"Uh, yes, detective, where were we?" She asked.

Even though her shapely features and pouting lips drew a strong seduction around McCall he kept shaking off his desire.

"The vial!" McCall snapped.

"We believe that there was one suspect that may have confiscated the container when it docked at our ports," she continued. "Chang was an ex-employee who never really gave us much trouble. His full name is Lou Chang and we lost his location in Chinatown a few weeks ago." McCall quickly wrote the name down in his private log. He was doubtful about the whole case now that Lou Chang's name was mentioned.

"Our lab discovered a liquid inside the vial," McCall continued. "Would you have any idea what it could be?" Nu began to squirm in her seat at his inquiry.

"We don't know for sure?" She replied with hesitation.

"Well, what did your scientist find so far?" McCall asked.

"Although the substance was well preserved my team still can't figure out what it may have been use for?" Nu continued.

"We are still missing some of the Huang's scroll which is still buried with the timber ships under the ocean."

"Can you tell me anymore about some of the artifacts you've already found?" McCall replied.

"There was a peculiar passage written upon the relief's. It was about a plant Chao Huang discovered. Apparently he found its' sustenance to be very useful. There was one script about, tsung-di, written on some timber planks that we've recently dug up. The script explained some healing remedies that were once widespread all throughout the ancient region of China." Nu Shangxi explained and McCall began to soak in all the facts. Some of the pieces began to fit together for McCall but there was one piece that was still missing.

"Our forensics team has decoded some of the elaborate etchings on the vial too," McCall stated proudly. "However some of our test's exposed that the chemical had a similar relation to opiate." Nu Continued.

"I wish I could tell you more, detective, but I have no more time to spend with you right now." She replied. She handed the vial back to the detective. McCall wasn't buying her story. Chao Huang may used an opiate-like substance to heal his ancient community but McCall believed that she may be hiding something else behind the dig.

"Very interesting information Miss Shangxi and all too fascinating for me," McCall returned. "But I really came here to ask you a more important question,"

"And what more do you need to know detective?" She replied.

"I wondered if you might know two men, Edward James or Angel Vasquez?"

"No, who are they?" Nu Shang asked.

"They were apart of the shooting at Jackson heights a week ago the same place I found the vial. One is a victim and the other is a suspect." McCall fired at Nu Shangxi.

"Sorry, I do not know him or anything about the matter." Nu said. Her hand quickly slipped under the desk and pressed a hidden security button. She then gently opened a hidden file drawer beside the desk and retrieved a photo. Lou Chang appeared in the photos.

"Here," she Commanded. "Take these." McCall grew with interest over the profile of Lou Chang after she handed black & white proofs over to the detective.

"We still don't have enough evidence on who gunned down Eddy James the night of the shooting and," McCall stated.

"What are you trying to state, detective?" She returned.

"Unfortunately, Miss Shangxi, you may under suspicion." McCall returned.

Nu Shangxi grew with disbelief and a look of apathy came upon McCall as he prepared to give her the bad news. Behind her meek facial expressions there still was an air of despondency with her stately character. Nu rose to her feet with confidence and somehow she still kept her composure around the detective. Two armed security guards quietly entered the office and they passed behind McCall. The detective heard a creak in the floor and jumped around to face them. Nu slowly approached him with a dark intention in her eyes.

"I may know nothing of what goes on in the streets, detective, but the photos I gave you should be a clue as to where you should start."

"Don't play games with me, Miss Shangxi, I need more answers." McCall replied.

"I assure you if you find who has the stolen container you'll find your answers." He continued. "We have reason to believe that Lou Chang may have contact with a triad that call themselves the Fists."

"The Fists, tell me how do you know of them, Miss Shangxi?" McCall asked sharply. A new light emerged on the case. McCall knew the Opium King had many slimy dealings with the Fists and Nu Shangxi had ties to them. Her image as a proud owner of Yangtze Shipping was now looking suspicious all the more. Nu's stare remained upon the detectives suspicious glances.

"He may plan to sell the container to them and we would be much obliged that you find Lou Chang before he sells it." She insisted while shifting files around her desk nervously.

"Well, when we do find Chang we will notify you." McCall replied. Nu look upon McCall with a dark stare and in return his attention was draw back to her. He was geared for more information from Nu.

"What I am about to tell you is off the record, detective, the Fists attempted to rob my family's import business years ago." She explained carefully.

"What trouble did they cause you, Miss Shangxi?" McCall injected.

"They tried to take over the warehouse and kidnapped me and my brother. He was shot to death in the middle of gun play."

"This is the first of my knowledge of this place ever being robbed?" Said McCall.

"My father eventually stopped them and we've had no more trouble with them since." She sighed. "But it wasn't until the last break-in in the warehouse did I suspect them again."

"On the record or off the record, Miss Shangxi, this still doesn't leave you off the hook." McCall stood before her arrogantly.

"I see," she said carefully. "There are however something's, detective, that are better left unsaid," She suddenly drew close to McCall. "Especially for the safety of your own life." Nu kept glaring at McCall. He was stepping into deeper waters with Nu and she may have been a prisoner of the Fists but he couldn't prove that now. McCall understood that the investigations of her secret dealings would have to be postponed and finding Lou Chang would help to solve some current riddles that were obstructing his suspicions of her.

"I'll take your word for it now but if I find anything else connected to the shooting you might be going down as well, Miss Shangxi." Threatened McCall.

"Well, you must be leaving me now." She instructed.

"I have some business to attend today." McCall could feel the shakiness in her voice and he knew there was something more that Nu Shangxi was hiding. The two armed guards gripped McCall's extremities and began to tear him away from the conversation.

"Hey, call off your dogs, I know the way out." McCall replied shoving the security guard back.

"We must meet again, McCall." She returned conceitedly while closing the door behind her. The two guards picked up McCall then escorted him outside of the building. He was a bit shell shocked over the matter but remained calm even though they accosted him with brute force. Nu's action's changed the opinions McCall had of her. He knew she may be hiding more than just family secrets.

Chapter 11: Suspects

NU WAS GETTING QUITE NERVOUS about the detective presence. She felt he was getting too close. A mysterious man entered the office Sung Jinn appeared. He was nearly seven-foot tall with Mongolian-like facial features. He had scars from shrapnel fall out during past civil wars serving as a red guard in China but now he served as a contract killer for Nu Shangxi.

"Sung Jinn, follow the detective. I feel he's a bit nosey." She commanded.

"What could he know?" Jinn asked.

"He had brought something of interest to my attention." She continued. "Follow him and get to Lou Chang before the detective."

"Why do you want me to follow this Yankee detective?" Jinn asked.

"Well, we don't want Lou Chang telling the detective too much information about our business!" She implied. Jinn nodded in agreement with her then quickly disappeared.

Back at the police station...

Now that he found a new suspect, McCall, went back to the precinct tracking down Lou Chang's criminal files at a late hour. He began to finger through a few files that were lingering between heaps of paper work at his desk.

"Damn!"

No dirt was found on Lou Chang, except a few parking tickets. One ticket was recently given to him at the corner of a drug store in Chinatown and it was McCall's lucky day. Lou Chang's silver import was obstructing the drug store on the corner during the hours of midnight and three o'clock pm.

McCall began to think to himself.. "If Lou Chang has been seen in the vicinity of Chinatown recently then finding him was going to be easier than planned."

McCall started to pack up some surveillance gear into the car before he left. Finally his unmarked cruiser pulled into a vacant alley way behind the drug store. He walked across the street and hid. Night crept in and storm clouds began to settle over Chinatown. The sky seemed to have grown darker from the coming storm and visibility got worse for McCall's stakeout.

"He won't be coming here anytime soon, I knew it." McCall thought as he climbed back into his car.

He slowly turned the engine over in his car and then another car appeared out of the blankness of the night. It was pulling in front of the drug store. McCall rolled down his window to get a better look. The rain was too heavy for him to see. He then jumped out of his car to get a better look. The rain beat down steadily on McCall while standing in the street. Even though it was too hard to see anybody moving in the dark, McCall caught the glimpse of a silhouette. His image seemed to fade in and out of the stormy night. The cold rain sent him a chill but McCall was driven to find whereabouts of Lou Chang. The car fit the description of Chang's vehicle and the license plate had matching numbers. McCall search seemed to be ended at the drug store but there was something blocking the path of justice. He scanned the building for a way to the apartment above the store and the fire escape. While the rain beat down steadily he trudged through the wet trash bags and grappled a fire escape safely. A door opened up, as he was half way up the latter. A shadowy figure fled down the fire escape.

"Hey, you, stop there, police!" He kept calling aloud but no matter how loud his voice was the rain kept stifling his voice. The suspect made a clean get away. McCall then rushed down to his unmarked police cruiser and chased after him. The chase lasted nearly an hour and he had lost the car down the interstate ramp heading north.

Chapter 12: The Cathedral

12:00 P.M..

ACROSS THE CITY THE MID-DAY sun was now glistening over the city buildings. Eddy was busy on his shift busing people to their jobs when a distressed woman hopped into his cab.

"Where to miss?" Eddy mumbled.

"To the cathedral." She whimpered.

The cab ride wasn't too far away. A few turns through traffic and they were there. Eddy parked across the street and the woman climbed out. Eddy began to stare aimlessly at the cathedral's massive stoned arches while she waited patiently for him to give her the rate. Viewing architecture was something of a delicacy to Eddy and most city's tourists.

"How much, sir?" Asked the sobbing female.

She asked wiping the tears that streamed down her face. His attention was strangely drawn to the distressed woman. Eddy gazed upon her with some remorse and his eyes seemed dropped low with guilt while she stood crying silently.

"Don't worry about the money, miss." Eddy replied. She thanked him then vanished into the cathedral.

A memory began to surface as Eddy remembered cleaning the church steps at the age of fifteen. He spent most of his youth living around the church. There he learned about God and discipline. He evened remembered living in at the orphanage just a block away from the church. It was a tragic day however when Eddy decided to flee the the church to become a hood. Vasquez was an early childhood friend who had boosted a car and that very same day and something changed in Eddy when he noticed the wildness in Vasquez's eyes. He felt he wanted to be free too but Eddy's choice came with a price. Since then he never looked back upon his last decision to leave the church with Angel. The cathedral seemed to remain even though Eddy was now a social recluse. He wandered too far as an adult from a pious life. Often he wondered would it be different if he had stayed at the church? Maybe he would've become some sort of priest or a minister? Who knew? However it was a miracle that he even survived his past.

Finally, he decided to enter the cathedral to say a prayer. He picked out a back pew, genuflected and then sat down. His head bowed in silence and prayed for his soul. Upon opening his eyes a jovial priest appeared grinning beside him. Eddy's eyes brightened at the sight of Father Wickabee. He was a shrinking older man with big round eyes that always wore half a grin. He was from British Isles and was commissioned to the cathedral in New York City shortly after the great war. Father Wickabea had been there ever since. Eddy even remembered him from his first day of school, when he had blessed the children one day.

"Where have you been, Edward?" The old priest placed his withered hand on Eddy's shoulder gently.

"Hello, father."

"Did the world capture you my son?" He whispered with a grin.

"I'm afraid so, Father?" Eddy slightly bowed his head.

"Don't let pity keep you away. I'm always here." He calmly turned half way like a doting guardian.

"By the way don't forget to say your prayers." He remarked sharply then looked upon Eddy with compassion and gave him a bit of his wisdom. He knew Eddy to be the average sinner but he never once rejected him when he came to say a prayer. Father Wickabea left him and Eddy was now alone with his thoughts again. But a question began to arise while Eddy sat and reflected upon his desolate lifestyle.

Why was I left here to embrace life alone? Eddy couldn't seem to answer his own tragic thoughts. Only memories of humble beginnings could be an answer. He began to remember the stench of the alley where he was once abandoned. The odor still seemed to ting his olfactory senses with the smell of refuse every time he remembered the place. It was on a dark night in nineteen hundred and eighty six, when Eddy was abandoned. He was only four years old. The nuns told Edward, his father was a husky man, nearly forty years old and he left the boy alone with only a letter. Eddy kept the letter close to him at all times. He read it often to himself every night.

It read:

"I am ashamed and I have no place for this child. Please look upon him with your mercy. Thank you."

Initialed J.T. The letter was so vague that it didn't even mention Eddy's true name. Eddy was one of the many abandoned youths that church took in. The clergy had baptized him, Edward James, after one of the late patriarchs of the community.

He left the church amid his frustrations with a better spirit after a short embrace with his faith. He hit the street again and turned down the off ramp heading to Mr. Li's garage. A traffic light suddenly flashed red and Eddy slammed on the brakes hard.

"Damn!" He screamed.

The passenger door opened mysteriously then closed. Eddy caught a glimpse of the stranger's long blonde hair in the rear view mirror.

"Look, I'm off the clock," he replied while turning around and to his surprise, Pandora, appeared. The late night lover couldn't get enough of him. The option to risk his limb again loomed over his consciousness but it didn't change his mind. Her red pouting lips quickly met with him and his fears were almost forgotten. Eddy felt that another throw with Pandora wouldn't change a thing with Switchblade. Eddy finally grinned at the idea of her nakedness would be in his grasp again then she smiled with delight too. His spiritual Mecca became something of the past since his soul was now burning with decadence.

Chapter 13: Last Thrill

The night rolled in Eddy's bed burnt with another erotic night. Pandora lie next to him partly naked and aimlessly twirling her curls around her fingers.

"Mickey always took my money from dancing but a smut like me couldn't do much to killer like Switchblade." Pandora cried to Eddy.

"I took all the violence he could give the other night at outside the bar." Eddy returned. The fiery night came quickly and he was feeling careless. The evening was drawn into several hours of passion and amid the lusting, ignorance grew between them during a dangerous hour and suddenly a dark shadow was cast over the apartment window. A strange man appeared in the night and remained there watching them have sex for a few moments. The moon light shined off his blade as it flicked open. He kept watching them as forbidden pleasure unfolded before his cross-eyes.

"Eddy would pay this time, pain-for-pleasure," Switchblade said in a whisper. Switchblade readied strike the glass with the end of his revolver.

"CRASH!"

A window exploded across their naked bodies just before Eddy could *get-off.* Glass shards were strewn all over the bed and some cut into Pandora's supple body. Switchblade then hovered over Eddy with a grimaced look.

"Are you ready to die?" He cackled at them. His blade slashed Eddy first spilling blood from his cheek then Switchblade began to slash Pandora's legs.

"This won't solve anything!" Pandora kept shouting.

"What do you want with me?" Eddy replied holding his bloody cheek.

"What do you people do all day while I'm out working, f*ck,?" he continued. "This must end." Switchblade then pulled out his 9 mm then cocked it.

"Ready to die?"

"Bang-Bang!" Two shots fired into the darkness like nightly fireworks.

Switchblade kept shooting at Eddy's legs until the bullet holes were showing through his skin.

"Ugh!" Eddy lamented with pain. Their bodies were now limp and lifeless.

"You thought you were going to get away with this one, eh"

He and two of the men put them into an unmarked van bound and gagged. Beating Eddy outside the bar wasn't enough for Switchblade but tonight Switchblade would make it right. He drove Pandora and Eddy to an abandoned warehouse. They were quickly pulled out of van and shortly after a cell door opened. Eddy was just waking up and he noticed the dusty concrete walls before Switchblade's men dropped them the same vacant cell.

"Well, if isn't Don Juan and his late night lover?" Switchblade said in anger and then he spat upon them.

"Go and get me some chains, Bruno!" Commanded Switchblade.

"Why are you doing this, Mickey?" Cried Eddy.

"Why you ask? Premise, it goes without saying."

“This doesn’t have to go any further.” Eddy replied.

“I told you never to sleep with her!” Switchblade yelled.

“She came on to me.” Eddy pleaded with Switchblade.

“This is between me and you.”

“I respected you enough, Mickey.”

“Respect, you didn’t really earn any of my respect.”

“You forgot all the jobs I did for you, Mickey, when I was a Dragon.”

“Those days are over and so are you,” he said then placed against Eddy’s temple.

“What are you trying to do, man?”

“You’ll see, Bruno, where are my chains?” Shouted Switchblade.

“Here!” Bruno threw the chains across the concrete floor and they landed by Switchblades feet.

Before he chained them he began to scourge Eddy’s open wounds with a whip and even pissed on him. Eddy kept writhing in pain while clinging to the wall of the cell.

“How long do think it was going to last?” Switchblade kicked in Eddy’s ribs but he didn’t move.

“Stop!” Pandora moaned at Switchblade. Eddy was now unconscious from the pain. Then Switchblade gazed upon Pandora’s bloody face.

“Why do I even care about her,” Switchblade cried. “Whores are a dime a dozen.” Switchblade replied.

“I may be a whore but you’re slime!” She spat back at him.

Switchblade gnashed on his yellow teeth then gave her a sharp backhand. One of his rings caught her left cheek which cut opened the other side of her mouth. She started bleeding on the floor.

“You bastard.”

“And as for you,” he suddenly got closer to Eddy and wielded a blade swinging it around threateningly.

"You'll get the works, cocky little SOB!"

Switchblade aimed his stiletto at Eddy's lower extremity and then pushed the knife through his jeans. Eddy began to cringe at the fine blade place at his testicles. Switchblade then laughed demoniacally. Bruno suddenly called down to Switchblade from above the concrete pit. He looked up at him while his hand remained upon Eddy's throat.

"Hey, Switchblade," he yelled. "We got company!"

"I'll be back for you both!" Switchblade warned then disappeared up the latter and headed up to the bar.

Chater 14: John and Martha

Out West...

John was an old truck driver that resided with his wife, Martha, in a quiet suburb of Wichita, Kansas but ever since a horrifying spill with his tractor-trailer John retired from driving big rigs across the states. He finally hung up the keys at fifty-eight. Martha always took care of the house and looked after him while he was bed ridden. They never left each other, especially in times of tragedy. Martha was there when John's body was nearly crushed under a rig that accidentally flipped a truck over on route. She stayed with him for weeks at the hospital until he was back to health. It took years for him to heal and after many surgeries he finally came out of his tragedy. His heart however suffered damage while he was under the wreckage of the rig. A heart attack struck while he was pinned between the roof of the truck and the driver's seat. They exhumed him from the rig safely and placed him in a hospital just in time to save him from injuries. The team of medical doctors knew that his heart wouldn't last into the coming years. One of his arteries of his heart collapsed as result of the accident. The medical doctors planned for him to have a transplant in a few years time.

Unfortunately, he would need to wait for a donor heart and times were grim for such an operation. John's quest for a new heart would keep him bed ridden at times and he mostly was weak. October rolled in and it was a month that a past trauma entered John's life. He visited the graves at a local cemetery mourning his very first wife, Helen, who died thirty-eight years ago. He met her on route in the early seventies at a diner called *The Lucky Stop.* His memory of her was recalled when they were once young single and in love. Eventually, he married Helen and the first few months of marriage was a dream. But John's long hours working on the road finally wore on their relationship and they began to fall apart.

Consequently, John was only married to Helen for only a few years. She couldn't take John's absence while he was on the road hauling paper products. A divorce date was set and the marriage was quickly over. Helen married Donald. She had a child with Donald after her first marriage ended but the child was left to John's care after she and her husband had been killed by a wreckless driver. Helen named him Jason. John had no time to foster the young, Jason, and there was no motherly figure to raise him. Eventually Jason had to be given up when he was only a few years old. In the year '80 John left him at a New York city church orphanage while passing a shipment through New York City and never looked back. The boy was a victim of circumstance and there was nothing else John could do. Years later Martha had given birth to a baby girl. They named her Emily. John wanted to raise Emmy right and later she became a successful businesswoman. John thought of the orphan boy from time to time but he never once tried to reach him.

John's life took a different path after Helen passed. His trucking business got bigger and better and could make time for his new wife. The unstable career as a trucker kept him single for a long time. He was involved with a girl that he met on route. Her name was Jaclyn and he had met her at a gas stop in Kansas during a snowstorm. And they fell in love immediately. She was convenient and it kept him from loneliness. Jaclyn however kept a low profile and didn't tell John everything about her past. She was hiding a previous marriage. She left her husband home, hopped into John's rig and never looked back. Years went by and John finally settled back in Kansas with Jaclyn. He had finally saved enough money to buy a home. And he even took a small job as shipping agent to spend more time with her. He pulled up to his house one late afternoon and noticed Jaclyn leaving with another man. They lived there for nearly three years before Jaclyn's husband finally found where she was living.

"Where are you going, Jaclyn?" John asked.

She never once answered him back before she left him. Her feelings for John changed suddenly and she couldn't verbally communicate with him. John sat back and watch Jaclyn kept packing her things into another man's car. He always had a feeling that a girl that young would eventually leave one day. John wasn't angry or emotional about her departure. He knew how she was, just a stranger he once knew. John had met her on rocky ground anyway and that was the way she left him. Another five years went by and the pain of loneliness crept in. Love wasn't much of friend to him over the years. Finally he sold the house that he had bought for marriage with Jaclyn. He moved to New York and the trucking business was calling again. He began hauling paper products around upstate New York. The job offered him over a hundred grand a year to start plus the big bonus.

While hauling paper goods to upstate New York he pulled into a gas station that was settled in a small hill town in the Adirondack's. There he met Martha working a register. Martha was then a brunette beauty that lived on a mountain ranch with her folks before she met John. She was only twenty-nine when he met her. John was approaching fifty then. She was a little shy and John was a little rugged from life on the road but they fell in love quickly. It wasn't long before they both settled down together. After five years of marriage Emily was born into their life. John stayed local and drove a bread truck to support their humble life-style and Martha raised Emily. Their life seemed easy until another tragic heart attack struck John.

Chapter 15: Tragedy Strikes

A MAN DRESSED IN A lab coat strutted out into the room. "Martha Smithton?" The doctor called as he read her name from the list.

"Doctor, I'm over here." She exclaimed. He swiftly walked over to her.

"How are you today, Martha?" He greeted her warmly.

"Fine," she responded. "I just want to know how John's doing?" She looked upon him impatiently.

"He needs to stay over a few nights." He instructed. "The doctors want to watch over his vitals over the night."

"Did they find anything?" She asked softly. The doctor's head dropped low and he flipped through the file on the clipboard.

"I didn't want to alarm you," he said. "They might have to do a surgery to keep one of the main arteries in the heart working until we could find him a new heart."

"Oh dear," she cried softly. "What are the chances that we could find him the right donor?"

"Well, chances are slim," he warned. "Martha, I will tell you that. It might be best to prepare." He fixed a gloomy stare upon her. And she looked back grimly for she knew what the doctor meant.

"He may live only a few short years after this surgery." He claimed contritely. She held her hand closed to her face in agony then turned away from him.

"Excuse me." The doctor then stepped aside in a respectful manner as she rose with tear-filled eyes and fled to the bathroom. Her life with John flashed before her eyes, while she cried alone in a stall. Twenty-eight years married with John didn't seem long enough. After some tears she called, Emily, her daughter about the bad news. Emily rushed to hospital from out west. Her job had taken around the globe as a researched for the environment. A few days went by and Emily and Martha finally were able to see John.

"How you doing, honey?" Asked Martha in a shaken voice?" John lifted his head a bit to get a better look at Martha.

"Fine, dear, I'm fine. Where is she?" Emily answered then propped her head beside Martha. She kissed his forehead with tears while they remained hovered over John.

"What's the matter with you?" John asked.

"I don't know, daddy?"

"You should know better, Emily, I'm no quitter." John proudly stated. She laughed in spite of her tears.

"How's the job? I know they have you flying everywhere." John asked impatiently.

"My company is flying me out to Hong Kong in a few weeks to evaluate the pollution problems in their cities." She explained.

"Wow, that's very interesting, Emily." John exclaimed. The doctor stormed into the hospital room and cleared his throat.

"Excuse me folks, I have to do a routine check up on John's machines here and you are welcome to come back in a few hours." The doctor said. Emily stepped away from his bed and looked upon her father with sorrow. She knew the doctors have been searching every region in the United States for John's donor heart and they all said the same thing. *"Good luck finding one."* He would be left waiting on the hook for a new heart for a very long time.

Back at the warehouse...

Some hours passed and Eddy began to awaken his eyes. He was longing for death that every moment pain emerged from his wounds. He felt that he was answering for his godlessness. However, death would eventually come from a more godless man than himself but for now it didn't bother him now. He knew he lived life to the fullest and there wasn't anything else left to live for. He noticed his legs while looking down upon them and was mesmerized at the amounts of gore spewing from the wounds. The pain was enough to kill him right then but he was still breathing. His broken sinews were shown through the scarred skin and he couldn't bear the sight of himself. He found Pandora but she was passed out in a pool of her own blood.

Consequently, Switchblade was still tied up with a shipment of opium that was hijacked by the police. He was trying to pull things together before another sting struck his operation.

"Damn," he said while passing over the new information files. McCall's journal was accurate and the FBI found the Opium King's operator across seas. Switchblade had to plan an new escape for the next drug bust to hit his bar.

"Wait till I get my hands on McCall. The police know everything now." Switchblade Exclaimed with frustration.

"What do you want us to do now, boss?" Asked one of his meandering thugs.

"I want you and Manny to grab a few guys scope out the north of the city here and prepare for any pigs that may arrive soon." Switchblade commanded. A waitress from the bar entered Switchblade's office.

"Angel Vasquez's here to see you." She said.

"Show him in the room."

Vasquez walked into Switchblades office with the box stuffed in a brown bag.

"What do you want now?" Growled Switchblade.

"Business." Snapped Vasquez.

"Business, eh?" Switchblade inquired back.

"Remember," Vasquez warned. "That deal we talked about last week?"

"Things are getting little too tight around here to do any new business, Vasquez."

"I heard about what happened to the lab?" Vasquez had worn deep concern upon his expressions. Switchblade's brow wrinkled with discernment over his knowledge of the break in.

"How do you know about the lab?" Barked Switchblade.

"Word gets around easy in the city about you." Continued Vasquez.

"I can't talk much about what happened the Feds are all around me now." Switchblade continued. He glanced around at the four corners of the room with a look of severity then fixed a heavy stare upon Vasquez.

"You know what I mean?" Replied Switchblade. Vasquez then nodded back to him.

"For now let's talk about this drug you stole from those triads." Vasquez quickly emptied its contents onto his desk. The vials and the ancient syringe appeared.

"You still want in on it, eh?" Replied Vasquez.

"I'll give you ten grand for it." Switchblade wagered.

"Ten grand," Vasquez said with disbelief. "I thought the deal was fifty, plus half of what you sell in the streets."

"Well, now aren't you getting a little too cocky, Vasquez." Advised Switchblade.

"That's a load of bull." Returned Vasquez angrily to Switchblade.

"No one else is going to offer you any more than ten grand on the streets." Switchblade implied.

"Maybe, but you're never going to see something like this ever again." Vasquez argued back.

"What makes it so different, then?" Asked Switchblade in doubt.

"I'm not like the other guys on the street Switchblade I can be trusted," continued Vasquez. "Those other guys you use are nothing!"

"I think you're lying and I don't take lightly to those who cross me!" Switchblade said. He knew Vasquez's loyalties were to be so desired and he proceeded the discussion with caution.

"What do you mean?" Asked Vasquez.

"I'll show you what I mean." Returned Switchblade.

Switchblade pulled out a remote and clicked on a nearby TV monitor. Eddy was shown chained to a wall bludgeoned. Vasquez rose and studied the TV screen carefully.

"That's Eddy, why is he all beat up?" He exclaimed.

"That's your boy who betrayed me by sleeping with my girl." Switchblade said with darkness in his eyes.

"You sick SOB!" Vasquez turned away from the screen and began to stuff the box back into his bag." He noticed Pandora passed out next to him and he began to realize why Eddy was all bruised up.

"I told him never to mess with her," Vasquez cried out.

"Evidently, he doesn't listen." Switchblade replied smartly.

"I never messed with her, Switchblade, I swear!" Vasquez implied.

"Are we settled at ten grand then?" Switchblade asked. He knew Vasquez attention was still fixed on Eddy's bloody image and capitalized on it.

"Look, Mickey, we'll be in contact." Vasquez rose nervously and began to stumble out of Switchblade's office. He realized that Eddy had gotten into deep waters with Switchblade after witnessing Eddy's bludgeoned face.

Chapter 16: Solitary

Across the city..

McCall planned another stake out in Chinatown in hopes to find Lou Chang. He set up in an apartment across the street from the drug store and dug in for a few hours. He waited all night for the right import to pass again but there was no sign of the vehicle. The night sky drew in and among the shadows of midnight the deadly assassin, Sung Jinn, appeared lurking about the apartment complex. The former red-guard was sent to scope out McCall because Nu Shangxi didn't trust the police and more important she didn't want him to find out her secret dealings with the Fists. Sung Jinn became her equalizer for McCall and the NYPD. McCall finally decided to investigate Lou Chang's apartment. He broke the lock open within a few seconds with an air can and a pick. He entered the apartment with ease and entered. The room was small and dark and it contained strong odors of incense and the musk tinged McCall's nostrils. He fumbled around until he tripped over a small end table covered with a mess of papers. He picked up the top note and began to read. He placed his flashlight placed over the pile of papers and began to rifle through them. The top note was fresh with ink and a location was written on it: Vasquez, Chinatown. "The East End" 8:00 PM January, 28th.

"Lou Chang had been networking for the lost box." McCall thought to himself.

McCall flashed a picture of the date in his mind then wrote it down.

"The East End, January, that's weeks from now?" McCall said to himself while placing the new clues together in his thoughts.

Suddenly the wind rattled the window then a shadow flashed across it. McCall jumped in hesitation, flicked off his flashlight and ducked out of the apartment. He held tightly to the fire escape and kept a low profile while he listened to footsteps growing closer to Chang's apartment. A mysterious figure appeared trying to enter the apartment through a nearby window. McCall noticed Sung's seven-foot-tall shadow along the outside door. He crept closer to the window and peered inside. A glimpse of the man's Asian features surfaced from out of the dark night. He stood by window's ledge and waited for figure to leave the apartment. Moments went by and there was no sign of him. It appeared to McCall that the giant man suddenly vanished.

The next day...

McCall was found at the precinct filling in a new report on the previous night. Captain Davis hovered over him like usual. He began to fix a heavy stare upon McCall.

"McCall," replied Davis. "Who is on your suspect list for today?" He looked up at the captain with a blank expression and paged through his thoughts.

"Nu Shangxi," he replied. "The owner of Yangtze shipping!"

"Tell me more!" Davis begged.

"She asked me to track down a thief she suspected as an former employee after I met with her over a piece of evidence." McCall continued. Davis picked up the file off McCall's desk and scanned through it.

"I feel that her former employee may have a connection to one of the shooters in the James case." Said McCall but he still didn't bother to mention the vial to Davis. He knew that the secret clue in the case did not fit together yet with the shooting and Davis didn't need to know. McCall's thoughts were placed back on Davis paging through the report.

"Nu Shangxi's ex-employee, eh," said Davis reading aloud. "Material Handler, Lou Chang, might be a suspect?"

"I still can't seem to finger his connection to the whole case." McCall grimly replied.

"Did you find anything else on him?" Asked Davis.

"He's still MIA," he continued. "Nothing turned up on him accept parking tickets." The captain paged through the case file and stopped at a particular page.

"Too many loop holes here, McCall," he replied. "We'd better re-evaluate the scenario beginning with the crime scene"

"I am still trying to fit it all together, captain."

"There had to be more than just one suspect here."

"The way things are developing in this case, captain, I am surprise that I was able to get anything out of Nu Shangxi." McCall remarked then Davis's eyes began to grow dimmer.

"Why, you think she's hiding things?" The captain asked.

"She has to be," he continued. "She told me of her father who had trouble with the city gang know as the Fists. We know they're always involved with some drug trafficking."

"Don't fool yourself, McCall, me and her old man have been friends for a long time before he past."

"No kidding, what were you two involved with?"

"We went boating together." The captain returned smartly.

"Don't ask stupid questions, McCall, just concentrate on the James shooting any more involvement with other cases can be dangerous." The captain seemed to be warning McCall not to dig deeper on NU Shangxi.

"She told me," McCall replied.

"Told you what, McCall?"

"She told me about her fathers past troubles with the drug lords." He said.

"That's all over now, we don't have to worry about that anymore." Davis replied.

"Then what should I do, captain?"

"As of right now I still need the interview with Eddy James for this case to be closed," he remarked. "or it will be clearly compromised by lack of information." Davis explained with authority.

"He didn't give me a sound statement the last time I visited the hospital." McCall said.

"Well, I suggest after you find this Lou Chang you should try questioning Eddy James again and close this case."

His stare upon McCall got heavier. "I'm counting on you, McCall."

"I won't let you down." McCall replied.

"Good!" Exclaimed the Captain then he turned and left McCall.

Chapter 17: East End Dive

THE NIGHT DREW IN OVER *The East End Bar* in Chinatown. McCall decided to scope out the place night before Lou Chang met for the box. He began to watch patiently for peculiar suspects passing among the crowded bar to see if this was a place Chang usually entertained. He decided to pace the floor in search for Lou Chang's mandarin features among the many faces in the bar but none matched the photo. He knew that finding Chang could end missing piece in the whole case but actually getting his hands on him may be more difficult then he imagined. Chang was a diamond in the rough and Chinatown was a sea of sand for likely suspects. McCall needed more time to put it all together but his time was falling short. Even though more suspects kept turning up in the case, he still needed Eddy's witness and finding Chang would end it all. McCall passed up and down the bar until the large bar crowd were down to only a few obnoxious drunks.

As the night drew on McCall began to get tired of waiting he finally called it quits. He stumbled to the lot, stepped into his car and fixed the rear view mirror. A shadow of a large man began to appear. McCall found him out of the rear view lurking behind his car. Uneasiness came over McCall so he jumped out from the car with his gun cocked. He started a search around the area with caution but the stranger disappeared into the darkness. Finally McCall hopped back into his car then sped off. The shadow of another car began to drag behind him along the highway. McCall stomped the brake petal and now he was behind the predator. The two cars broke the highway stripes and began to swerve in pursuit. Sparks began to fly while metal collided between cars. McCall snatched his radio and began to call in the plate number.

"Hello, does anyone copy?" McCall called over the CB radio.

"Copy." Returned the officer at the dispatch.

"I need you to scan a plate number."

"Go ahead."

"Late model, domestic, plate number DPD-123."

"Ten-four." The officer radioed back.

Suddenly the prowling Caddy swerved into oncoming traffic and McCall nearly lost the control of his Chevy. A few gunshot rang out that grazed the side of his car. Before he could return the fire the suspect had driven off.

"Damn!" He screamed while his fist hit the wheel.

The dispatcher radioed back to McCall. "It's stolen do you need assistance?"

"Don't bother, I got this one!" McCall replied over the CB.

He looked down at his watch and notice he was late for Taylor he knew she was waiting.

Taylor's House...

McCall finally pulled up to Taylor's house. The front door open at the sound of rattling keys. He walked into the room still vexed over the late night car chase while Taylor was dressed in a fine black dress. McCall's romantic thoughts were elsewhere that night. He placed his jacket in the closet then walked past the dinner table.

"Frank?" Replied Taylor. McCall was too busy grabbing a beer out of the fridge.

"Not tonight, Taylor, I've had a bad night." He answered coldly.

"What's the matter with you tonight, Frank?" Cried Taylor.

"Nothing!" He snapped at her then sat down to retire on the couch.

"Frank, why don't you come have dinner with me?" She begged. McCall glanced at the setting and sighed.

"That's a nice, honey, but after tonight,"

"-I was waiting up all night for you?" She replied. McCall realized that his current explanation for the late night was just another weak alibi.

"Never mind." He answered carelessly then began flicking through a few TV channels.

"I want to you to know how late you were tonight." She cried.

"Do you really want to know why I was late?" He replied in lieu of her nagging.

"Tell me." She answered.

"Fine." He shouted back.

"I was being chased down by psycho tonight on route." He explained with frustration.

"I think it's time you quit that job." Taylor replied.

"What do you mean," he said. "I found a man lurking around my stakeout in the city and it got a little dangerous and you need more proof," McCall swigged on more beer. "I can't just quit."

"You might not be able to make that decision, Frank," She continued. "But I know what I want for you." McCall's eyes dropped low and he tried to avoid her poignant stares upon him.

"Firstly, I don't want to see you in a casket and secondly, I want us to be safe." She explained.

"Things might get worse and I shouldn't stay the night." He replied. Taylor turned abruptly then walked to the closet and grabbed his jacket out of the closet. She shoved it into his hands.

"You know, Frank, I thought this would be a romantic night for both of us." She said in a shaken voice.

"A night for us?" McCall returned.

"Yes, the only night we had planned this year for the both of us."

"My head is spinning, I've been working on this case too long and I can't even get a minute to myself." He complained.

"What's stopping you from just quitting?" She snapped.

"You know I just can't."

"I make plenty of money for us to live on." She said. McCall rose in resentment beaming upon his brow. He slowly walked over to Taylor and put his arms around her. He began to stare deeply into her eyes and she waited for him to speak but there was silence between them. McCall knew her six-figure paycheck designing cloths was more than enough but he couldn't leave this case unsolved. His attention moved away from her soft green eyes with his dark uncertainty.

"I couldn't do that to you again." Said McCall. Taylor then pushed him away.

"You see you already did it," she began to cry with the aggravation for Franks affection. Tears continued to stream. "When we had this discussion last week you told me the same thing. I don't know what you even want anymore from me?"

"How could you say that, Frank?"

"What else do you need to know, Taylor?"

"I planned a dinner for us tonight because I believe we needed it but I feel we're falling apart." She replied. Her voice fell away from McCall's attention he knew that she was serious this time. McCall couldn't get his job off his mind to save his relationship with Taylor.

"Besides we're missing out on the good things, Frank." She continued.

"Taylor, I know but," Frank pulled her close and stared into her brown eyes. Taylor leaned into him and began to swoon.

"I can't let this case go, there's too much at stake." He replied. She pulled her hand away and stormed off to her bedroom door.

"Fine!" With one last cold stare Taylor slammed the bedroom door.

The next day...

A thundershower was forming outside the precinct windows while McCall was watching some video footage of the apartment hall video cameras. He watched carefully from his office window as the dark clouds swirled around. A police officer appeared wielding a document by McCall's door and he began to loathed the pile of casework that was incoming.

"The triads all look the same dressed in black in the monitors record. I can't decipher one different from the other." McCall thought to himself.

"Here you go, McCall, I got that beat on the domestic you wanted." The officer said handing the documents off to McCall.

"Already too late?" McCall said sarcastically then snatched the document from his hand.

"I really needed this information last night when the SOB was shooting at me on the expressway." McCall replied.

"Hey, it took a while it just came up stolen." The officer returned. McCall carefully studied the report.

"..The car was registered in Canada?"

"What maniac would come out of their way to hunt me down?" Thought McCall to himself.

Chapter 18: The Opium King

Eddy was still counting his blessings while lying in a concrete pit when Switchblade was suddenly called away from the states. He was sent to the shores of San Polo to meet with his superior, The Opium King. There the syndicate was preparing for the Feds and international authorities to storm their operation. The Opium King invited Switchblade to his private villa at San Polo to talk privately about the previous drug bust. It was a long ride and the plane finally landed on the remote island of San Palo, which was a two-mile-long island located off the coastline of South America. There, the Opium King's constituents greeted Switchblade and led him to a limousine. They climbed into the car and drove off for the villa. Switchblade greeted the Opium King after he was ushered out of the limousine. He appeared as a short and rotund man with Arab-European features. They hopped into an imported black Lincoln and drove up to the main mansion. The mansion lay at the top of a mountain he named little Olympia.

The mansion was a forty-four room villa with private pools on every floor, sitting on two hundred acres of mountainous soil and was well protected by over a thousand armed men. The Opium King did well for a drug lord but all was threatened now that he was in the eye of persecution. They walked through the oak doors of the mansion, entered the Opium King's main office and stood at attention. The main office was in the likeness of a twenties speakeasy. It was decked with elaborate marble bar-tops that ran the length of the office and dark walnut floors and neatly hung ruby red tapestries. Switchblade found a red velvet seat and settled his back into the lush padding.

"Two of my men spotted a strange man searching the island." He said as he propped his stubby legs on a Persian kneeler.

"Could it be the FBI?" Switchblade answered with suspicion.

"We are looking into it but for now I want you to freeze your operations in NYC?" The Opium King demanded in a calm voice.

"Boss, how am I going to keep things going?"

"I'll take care of your assets back in the states." He fixed a heavy stare upon Switchblade.

"But if I get wind that you still doing business behind my back I'll cut you off. And the sharks won't be as forgiving as I am, Mickey." Switchblade knew what he meant.

"Then what should I do in the mean time?" Cried Switchblade.

"Do what you do best tend bar like nothing happened." The Opium King snapped.

"We wouldn't want to bring any more attention to us now would we?"

"No." Remarked Switchblade. The Opium King rose and poured himself a glass of red wine.

"Come, all this talk has gotten me upset." Switchblade rose with him and a few of the guards they continued out to a veranda. He pushed open a set of atrium doors with pane glass. They led outside to a large white deck which nearly connected to the sky. The veranda was set purposefully on the high mountain with the small village below. The shrewd architecture gave a picturesque view of San polo's fishing islands and it all too cliché for a powerful drug lord's tastes for fine living.

"Hey, Boss, I have a mule in NYC who has come upon some new goods." Said Switchblade.

"Really, sounds like a small-time talk to me?"

"This drug drew in all the consumers around the city and more importantly the Fists are killing for it.

"The Fists? Will this new drug effect the business I have in the city?"

Switchblade's greedy eyes grew greener when he realized the Opium King insecurity was revealed.

"Well that depends?" returned Switchblade.

"How much do you want, Mickey?"

"One hundred million." Replied Switchblade.

"That's all?"

"And I want one of those small islands."

"Heh-heh, well see, my friend." The Opium King said amusingly.

"You give me his connection to the city and my operatives will handle it."

"When do I get the money?" Begged Switchblade.

"When I get the drug!" The Opium King returned.

Thunder struck over the valley and an overcast of a storm sent the party back inside. Dusk finally drew in and a native female servant led Switchblade to his chambers. He glanced out the canopy window and studied the new storm. Nighttime seemed darker after the storm as Switchblade turned in to rest. A light flickered among the darkness of the cloudy sky and he felt an uneasiness about the glimmering light. Switchblade began to study the light a little closer. And the sound of a helicopter vibrated the windows of his room he sighed and finally turned in for the night. He knew the island was being watched.

The moon finally sunk and the sun rose steadily above the island. Switchblade decided to walk the length of the island to shake off the tiredness of his sleep. He found a small path that led down the mountain and to the side of the sea. It was where the Opium King had built a private beach where some of the small village of drug mill workers took short siestas. The workers looked healthy and no ill will was in their eyes. The opium had taken care of them and the small village that he created. Some worked the docks and some ran the opium mills. The medical industry was a big supporter of the island and there wasn't anything else to do for money besides fishing. Overhead Switchblade noticed a plane hovering over the small airport built on the other side of the mountain. Two men in gray suits and sunshades climbed out of the twin-engine plane and they conveniently hop into a small car by the docks. He sped off racing back up the mountain path. He hopped out of the car in a rush and pushed through the mansion doors. He arrived at the main office and crept close to the half open door.

"How long have we've been doing business together?" Clamored the Opium King at the suspicious men.

"Twenty years," One of the men stated. "But Three Oceans Pharmaceutical is not going to take the heat for your illicit operation any longer." Exclaimed the other suited man in anger. The Opium King gnashed at the crowns of his teeth which nearly dissolved into dust at the sound of insolence.

"I'm the one that put your company on the map!" He continued.

"We understand that, sir, but.."

"You were once just a small time company when I found you. I kept you under my wings for very long and now all the industry wouldn't swear on another product that I produce." He said boldly.

"That was before we knew better." The business rep returned.

"Pretty soon the dogs are going to be crawling down our backs now because of the drug bust in the states." He cried.

"Nonsense." Said the Opium King.

"I merely cut all my financial ties with you and start a new lab." The Opium King continued.

"Are you insane?" The agent replied.

"And it's all legal." His eyes glowed with an interest of their fears of the international watchdogs.

"But your business is a gamble that three oceans isn't willing to take anymore how could you be strong enough to start with someone new?" Said the agent in stern voice.

"Well, what are you willing to risk?" The Opium King asked with a twitching eye.

"Your haphazard ways are uncouth and the company just can't hide our ties with you any longer."

"But you have no other choice." The Opium King argued arrogantly.

"No choice?" Objected the agent. "Do you have any idea what it takes to get international authorities off our back?" He cried.

"I told you don't worry about the watchdogs." He said with a fixed heavy brow.

"What happens when all the area's distributors shut down when they decide to investigate us? That's a clamp on one hundred forty billion dollars a year!" The agent screamed at the opium king.

"Please save your number crunching for tax season. I'll handle the situation and you can tell the senior brokers that everything will be fine." The Opium King commanded.

"I don't believe this." Said the agent in disgust.

"We can't be affiliated with a drug lord anymore they are on to us." The agent cried.

"Oh, I'm sorry our extra-marital affairs offend you but you need to see it my way, Fitz, show the boys out." The Opium King winked at one of his guards. One of the hefty men that guarded the mansion shuffled over to both agents and escorted them to their plane. Switchblade was alarmed at the conversation and he felt that the end was coming for the drug mogul. He watched as the plane slowly took flight but suddenly seconds later the blue sky was with fire and smoke. The Opium King wasn't satisfied with the conversation and he quickly took up vengeance upon them. With this action he would now take over as sole owner of the pharmaceutical company and there was no limit to his seat of power. Switchblade on the other hand sighed at the plane wreck and decided to cool off by the beach.

The Small Island..

Opium King would indeed run the business the way he wanted, crooked. The rejection by the agents of the three oceans pharmaceutical arose an air of suspicion in the Opium King. And he realized that, Three Oceans, called in the investigation. The island wasn't safe from the government and soon they would be climbing down the Opium Kings back. Before the sun dipped low into the horizon Switchblade decided to take a tour of the smaller islands before he got sent back to the muggy city. He took one of the speedboats out for a spin around Peqinos Ninos. They appeared smaller in size no bigger than a mile long. Two of which were covered by palm trees and uninhabited by the villagers. He sped around the last island that no bigger than a tiny hill which was only as long as a football field. He noticed a ring of smoke flying high up into the air. The smoke alerted his suspicions of who might be living there.

The sun was finally laying low and the night was about to settle in. He docked the boat at another side of the island and crept on to the mainland. There was a tiny dirt path that led into the lush jungle brush and he carefully hobbled down the path. He quickly realized a strange camp that was set up there along with a small satellite and a green camouflage tent. Switchblade was caught in suspicion over the encampment. Also there was fire cracking beside the tent and it appeared someone had just set up camp. A fear gripped Switchblade as he drew nearer to a campfire. He readily found his concealed .22 pistol then loaded the breach. A nearby palm gave him cover as he waited for the mysterious visitor.

He had remembered the helicopter that flew by the island the previous night and he had feeling that it was the rogue agent that was combing the island. He crept closer to the campfire and scanned the area but no one was in sight. Switchblade got closer to the camp and began to pick through the camp. Switchblade found some files and pictures of the island. It appeared to him that the man might only be a researcher or a scientist of some sort. A moment went by and a shadowy figure climbed out of the water carrying a string of fish with him. The stranger staggered upon a dirt path heading towards his camp. Then Switchblade backed out of the tent and haphazardly knocked over a pile of files which were placed at the edge of the tent. He quickly bent over and put them in place and noticed a FBI document among the research papers. A rustle in the jungle brush alerted him. Switchblade stormed out of the tent wielding the document and boarded his speedboat for the mansion. Switchblade barged into the mansion office and stood before the Opium King out of breath.

"What's the meaning of this?" He boomed. Switchblade raised the document before the drug lord.

"I found an agent!" Exclaimed Switchblade.

"An agent?" Asked the Opium King in suspicion.

"It looks as though he's camped out on the last island that's connects to the mainland." Said Switchblade nervously.

"How do you know for sure?" He continued calmly.

"Some of the natives fish only off that island."

"But he's not a native." Switchblade replied.

"What makes you think that, Switchblade?"

"I noticed a small helicopter flying overhead the previous night and then I found some smoke on the island. I arrived at his camp and along with the satellite dish I found this document among some phony looking research papers." Claimed Switchblade.

"Let me see it!" The Opium King commanded impatiently. Switchblade handed the document over to the Opium King and his eyes widened at the first sight of the information.

"It appeared he's has been studying our mill production and distribution ever since we began this operation."

Chapter 19: The Invasion

The new information sent the Opium King into a fever of anger and resentment. He had been ignorant with the whole operation and he knew his empire was about to end.

"He's been here for many months undetected." Said the Opium King with frustration.

"I've been lax in patrolling the whole chain of islands." He sighed.

A team of armed men hopped into speedboats and quickly swarmed the tiny islands in hope to find the agent. There appeared to be no escape for the unsuspecting agent however and no sooner would they find him. A few men stormed the last island and only found a desolate camp. The fire had been doused and the tent collapsed. He must have caught Switchblade impeding on his camp and fled. The search ended abruptly and the camp was abandoned. Two guards stayed behind to watch the island for his return and Switchblade turned in for the night.

The next day...

The sun finally peaked through the shades of Switchblade's room and he awoke suddenly with the cold steel of a gun poised between his eyebrows.

"W-what the-?" He mumbled while fixing himself before the strange man dressed in a suit.

"Who the hell are you?" He demanded.

"We followed you here from NYC." The American agent explained pulling out a pair of handcuffs.

"What the f*ck is this about?"

"It's your friend. We have reason to believe he fled for Hong Kong shortly before we arrived."

"You suits are relentless!" Switchblade complained.

A few days later...

With the Opium King's drug mill now under final investigation of the international supervision it was time to hit the local drug rings that he shipped drugs to from the island. The Purple Lady was the first bar to feel the sting. The swat team busted the bar doors wide open and a few of Switchblade's loyal men opened fire upon the swat team. The small gang of thugs could only stave off the invasion for a short time and the police eventually overwhelmed them. McCall was called to finalize some clues after the skirmish was over. He and two others broke into the underground lab and McCall found Eddy and Pandora clinging to life in the concrete bunker.

"Funny finding you here?" Chuckled McCall as he unchained Eddy from the concrete bunker.

"It took you guys long enough." Eddy returned.

"We got held up." McCall turned to the unconscious woman. Who's she?" Asked McCall.

"Only the lusty dancer in NYC, Pandora" Said Eddy while the EMT cleaned blood off of her face.

"Maybe you should find some where else to dance, this place is getting shut down." Said McCall.

"Enough with the advice, just get me out of here!" She moaned. McCall had a lot to deal with now that the case was blown open. Eddy's connection to the whole thing was now brewing new questions for McCall. Eddy however was left in the hospital after the doctor found fatal gunshot wounds had damaged his legs. Surgery took several hours to extract countless bullets from his body once again. A surgeon walked calmly into his hospital room toting a clipboard.

"How do you feel today, Edward?" Asked the doctor sincerely.

"I feel like someone danced on my legs with hot lead and didn't bother to give me a kiss good night." Said Eddy jokingly as he squirmed around on the bed. The surgeon looked gravely upon his suffering patient and sighed.

"You're lucky you didn't die this time!" He explained while jotting down a few notes.

"Will I ever be able to walk?" He asked with a shaken voice. The surgeon fixed a heavy stare upon Eddy and his question.

"You better rest up and we'll see in few weeks." Without another word the surgeon stormed out of the room leaving Eddy to his thoughts.

Chapter 20: Deadly Game

Now that the infamous *Purple Lady* had been seized and the drug mill busted the Opium King was finished. McCall could now further investigate Eddy's shooting. He walked through the elevator doors and into the hospital room once more to meet with Eddy. McCall stopped abruptly at the entrance of his room and watched silently while a day nurse tended to Eddy's scars. McCall was hoping for answers.

"How's it going?" McCall asked innocently as the detective eased into the room. Eddy turned towards McCall then he fiddled with a control for the bed.

"Fine, just fine but I got shot again." Laughed Eddy.

"Hey, it could be worse." McCall joked then crept closer to the hospital bed and stooped over him.

"Could we talk a little?" McCall was hesitant about Eddy's reaction.

"What about?" Snapped Eddy.

"About the shooting that happened a few months ago!" McCall ejaculated.

"Well, now that I know you're really a cop. I think I could trust you this time." He replied.

"So, it's a trust thing?" McCall returned mockingly.

"You know the streets you can't trust anyone." He looked up at McCall and waited for his answer.

"I know the streets all too well." Returned McCall.

"Pull up a chair!" Commanded Eddy. McCall quickly found a chair with ease then sat down.

"Where do we begin?" Eddy opened.

"Should we start with your past involvement with the Dragons?" Eddy suddenly lost of composure over McCall's interrogation.

"I'm not a gang-banger anymore." He argued with McCall.

"Explained your involvement with the Fists then." Asked McCall.

"You got a cigarette?" Interrupted Eddy.

"No, I don't smoke." Said McCall.

There was a brief silence in the room. Eddy kept stalling to evade McCall's previous question. Finally he spoke up.

"You might think Fists busted the door down in my apartment," he continued. "But it wasn't them. I bumped into Vasquez recently. The group of men busting into my apartment were triads looking for something Vasquez stole from them."

"This sounds like new information." Said McCall excitedly.

"He thinks they may have been hired by the Shangxi family." Eddy was filling in the blanks for McCall and suspicions arose about Nu Shangxi unclean character.

"Tell me, why?" Asked McCall chiseling for more answers to the unsolved mystery.

"They were looking for a stolen container." Claimed Eddy. McCall refrained from exposing his previous chat with Nu Shangxi over the artifact. He knew one word would ruin his confidence with Eddy.

"I read this week's newspaper on the article theft." He continued. "As far as I know Vasquez still has it in his possession."

"What does it look like?"

"It was a small box with a bunch of ancient script on it." Eddy explained.

"I couldn't believe I was shot over a cheap box!" Eddy continued.

"There's a little more to this riddle, my friend." McCall answered firmly then he pulled out pack cigarettes and stealthily handed them over to Eddy.

"I thought you didn't smoke?" Eddy replied.

"Don't freak out. I'm still on your side of the story, Eddy." He lit up a cigarette then gave it to Eddy.

"How did Vasquez wind up with this mystery box?" Asked McCall.

"Some bullshit story." Answered Eddy.

"I'm listening?" Replied McCall.

"You see.. the Fist's shot up another triad that owned alley way territories in Chinatown and the box was left behind." Eddy remarked.

"Vasquez said he snatched it from an alley way." He implied.

"There the drug inside the cheap box that made it an interesting item on the street." Eddy carefully described.

Chapter 21: Tsung-Di

Continued...

"What else did Vasquez say about this drug?" McCall asked.

"Vasquez said the peasant Chinese have a legends about the drug. They say it will make you like a dream with no end, *immortal*." Eddy replied.

"Heh, who would believe that bull?" Laughed McCall.

"But it does has a name around the city as a righteous drug." Replied Eddy.

"Likely story even for a guy like you to believe, eh, Eddy." Continued McCall with his cynicism. Eddy's eyes suddenly dropped low and he became uneasy then he looked up at McCall.

"I took the drug to get high just before the triads came." Replied Eddy. McCall began to remember the night of the shooting.

"Then it might be true after all and you're still alive?" McCall joked again.

"Vasquez thought it was just opiate or some type of heroine mixture but it was definitely something different." He continued.

"Where do you think Vasquez is now?" McCall popped another question that Eddy would've normally eluded.

"He could be anywhere." Replied Eddy.

"What do you think he might do with that drug in his possession?"

"I know he's attempting to produce the drug and sell it for big money." He continued.

"He's been all over the city looking for a buyer. You'll might find him in Chinatown."

McCall knew there was more to this story but Eddy gave him all that he would need to solve the case. The plight over the stolen box kept toying with McCall's consciousness and he felt that he was still missing a clue. The idea of the drug actually being a gate to immortality was a tempting fantasy to believe but in reality to McCall it was just a fable. Even though McCall was drawing at straws to put the case together Eddy gave McCall more evidence that Nu Shangxi was connected in the opium ring. He sensed that she may have a hand in shipping the raw material. After Eddy answered some questions McCall realized a new twist emerged now that Nu Shangxi was a suspect. She became the target of McCall's suspicions. The detective was engulfed over the possibility that Nu may take over the Opium King's territories. But only time would reveal her mysterious hand in the matter. McCall's focus now was to find Lou Chang.

Lou Chang...

Three weeks had passed and he was hot on the trail of Lou Chang. McCall had remembered the past stakeout by the drug store and he fingered through a copy of Lou Chang's notes. He matched the area locations and the date that Chang was to meet Vasquez. McCall found that Lou Chang was also hiding out among ruins of an old building in Chinatown, hiding from the Nu Shangxi's black hand. Chang had planned a rendezvous with Vasquez at a bar across town with Chang posing as a possible buyer for the box.

January 28th...

McCall waited patiently for the meeting to take place at a local city bar. Vasquez was passing through the streets of Chinatown before he met with Chang. He took his time and made a few deals before he arrived at the meeting spot.

"Third Street, The East End." Said McCall. McCall watched as Vasquez passed his unmarked cruiser and found him entering a local bar with a green dragon on the facade. McCall then decided to enter the bar shortly after Vasquez. He pulled up a seat, remained inconspicuous and calmly watched as two young Asian dikes went at it on stage. They caressed each other with lashing tongues as McCall watched while incognito. Vasquez however was pacing the bar for his contact. He stroked his goatee while in search of a seat. He scoped a nearby table and sat down by another man who McCall didn't recognize. He began to study the picture that Nu Shangxi gave him. The features of the peculiar man sitting with Vasquez seemed to match the characteristics of Lou Chang.

"Say," said Chang, "where is the box now?" Vasquez threw the petty thief a sinister look.

"It's somewhere safe." He replied. Vasquez's hand rose and signaled a waitress. She quickly appeared with two drinks.

"I give you five-thousand now and you give it back to me tonight." Chang replied in hesitation.

"Too cheap!" Vasquez sneered.

"But that container belongs to me," he said. "I am the one who had it first." Chang claimed.

"How so?" Vasquez returned in suspicion.

"Let's just say I had my hands on it when it arrived here." He implied with a dark stare then he turn his head around the bar with looks of curiosity as if someone was watching him.

"You're the notorious thief that was all over the papers today?" Vasquez replied with accuracy.

"You're lucky I offered you anything for it." Chang returned with a vengeful look.

"Now it's time for me to take it back." Chang said rising slowly. Vasquez jumped back in his seat as he noticed the barrel of a tiny gun poking from under Chang's sport jacket.

"You'll have to do a lot better than that, 'Ese?" Vasquez said arrogantly while clenching his fist.

Chapter 22: Bad Deal

A DRINK CRASHED ACROSS THE table and the grip loosed on Lou Chang's gun. Vasquez jumped for his throat and the two collided into a fistfight. McCall was quick to rise while the crowded bar began to entertain the fist fight.

"Break it up-" Commanded McCall while rifling through the fallout of the crowded fight. "NYPD!" McCall replied flashing his badge before the crowd. Vasquez's hands rose instinctively then Lou Chang quickly vanished out of the crowded bar.

"Don't move!" McCall ordered moving closer to Vasquez pushing aside the rest of the bar crowd.

"Damn!" Vasquez cursed after he knew his gig was up.

"Everyone remain calm!" McCall yelled at the rest of the crowd while he pushed aside Vasquez.

"Where did your buddy run too?" McCall inquired preparing his cuffs.

"I guess you weren't fast enough to catch him, eh?" Vasquez replied standing with raised arms.

"I'd watch your mouth." McCall snapped at him while he was placed in cuffs.

"You're a wanted man, Vasquez!" McCall replied now realizing Chang had slipped out of his grasp for good.

Back at the Station..

Vasquez was hauled back to the station for questioning and remained quiet for most of the trip. McCall found a nearby desk after they got settled. He pulled out a report file and a recorder. He began to prepped Vasquez for his statement.

"Planning something back at the bar, ESE?" McCall said as he read down Vasquez's criminal record.

"No," returned Vasquez. "We just had a little problem over the bill."

"C'mon, Vasquez," fired McCall, "I know you better than that?" He held a piercing stare over Vasquez.

"What were you two lovers really arguing over?"

Vasquez began to smirked upon McCall.

"Nothing that really concerns you!" He returned coldly.

"Really, was it another drug deal?" Asked McCall.

"You got nothing, copper!" Vasquez screamed placing his stare right back at him.

"Do you want to know why you're really here?" McCall said shoving the file in front of Vasquez.

"You have three accounts of armed robbery, attempted murder, and possession with the intent to sell." Recited McCall. "It had to be over something, tonight?"

"I have nothing to tell you," Vasquez remarked. "Besides I did my community service years ago." Vasquez in a fit of disgust pushed the pile of report across McCall's desk.

"Well-" Said McCall. "If you don't tell me something you'll get three more years in community service not to mention 10 years for the intent to sell?" McCall was resentfully this time. Vasquez realized that the detective was for real this time.

"Wait, Wait!" Vasquez replied again and again.

"How's that sound?"

"Okay, fine, I'll tell you that I was there to meet Lou Chang." He recounted to the detective.

"And what were you there meeting with Lou Chang for?" McCall inquired then shuffled his paper work around.

"I had something he wanted." Explained Vasquez.

"What could an migrant worker from Honk Kong want with you, Vasquez?" McCall then fixed a stare upon Vasquez that could melt led.

"He want a box." Vasquez returned sharply.

"Just a box, then why did your pal tell me you were going to mass-produce a drug?" McCall kept drilling at Vasquez for more information.

"Who did told you that? Vasquez asked.

"Wouldn't you like to know." McCall replied.

"Was is Mickey, he's just a sh*t faced liar!"

"No, but before I tell you where is the stolen container?" Asked McCall.

"I put it in a safe place for now."

"Something is just not fitting for me, ESE, and I am afraid to ask if you have anything to do with the stolen container from Yangtze shipping?" Vasquez turned away at McCall's cold and calculating stares.

"No, I actually found the box in?" Vasquez replied while eluding McCall's hard interrogation.

"The alley where the Fists owned the territory right?" McCall finished the rest of Vasquez's conversation. Vasquez began to grow nervous.

"Who's the snitch this time and he told you everything I bet?" This time Vasquez softened up a bit around McCall.

"You happened to leave your friend to die a couple of weeks ago in Queens." A disturbed look came over Vasquez's face.

"Are you feeling guilty yet?" McCall finally seemed to catch Vasquez's guilt.

"Eddy-" Vasquez cried out. "That damn burn-out!" McCall realized Vasquez desperation and he held tightly to the reigns to get the whole truth out of Vasquez.

"While we're on the subject," Vasquez continued.

"What else did Eddy happened to tell you?"

"It's on a need to know basis." McCall replied.

Another officer appeared with Vasquez's coat.

"I need to know?" McCall demanded. He then quickly turned to the officer and waited patiently for him to report.

"Does he have anything on him?" Asked McCall while he waited patiently.

"I search it and I found nothing on him." The officer returned then McCall sighed.

"He's clean, then?" Asked McCall to the officer.

"Whatever was inside the jacket he must take it out at the time of the arrest because he has no paraphernalia on him?" The officer returned sternly.

"McCall, By the way I have a few of those photos of Yangtze shipping docks like I asked you."

"Thanks officer."

"Anything else, detective?" Vasquez returned wisely.

"No." Said McCall in uneasiness over Vasquez's innocence.

"This isn't charity that happens often but you can leave now." Said McCall. Vasquez looked back upon McCall with doubt.

"Now scram!" The officer picked up Vasquez and released from his cuffs. He quickly disappeared out the precinct. It would only be a matter of time when Vasquez turned up again in the police beat. Vasquez spread around the city like the plague with a new deal and soon the truth would reveal the container. He knew there was more to the mystery of Eddy's shooting and the missing container had a bigger connection to Nu Shangxi.

Chapter 23: A Dangerous Suspect

The zenith of Nu Shangxi's otherworldly power was a silhouette lingering among the shadows of McCall's life. McCall had to do some more footwork to catch the slyness of the devil but until then evil was still lurking at the corners of the city.

Meanwhile...

It was about evening and Sun Jinn hopped out of his car with his 9mm and into the night. The moon lay now at the horizon line of the night sky in full yellow. He pushed through the thick brush until he reached a moon lit clearing. He arrived at a stone-faced colonial in the nook of a quiet suburb of New York. His eye caught a glance of a curvy silhouette dancing behind a set of taupe drapes. Blood lust quickly entered Sung's sanity for the moment and the grip on his pistol grew tighter. Sung Jinn wasn't just a killer but a disciplined assassin. He was clean and neat when he executed his victims and this job was no different then past jobs.

Taylor suddenly peeped through the curtains and Sun Jinn dove into the next lot of bushes. After a few moments of silence the lights finally went out in Taylor's house. It was time for Sung Jinn to enter. He shimmied the window's lock with a small file and set foot in the house. Slowly he crept up the stairs and arrived at the second floor hallway. He paused briefly and prepared a silencer. He poked his gun into a few empty rooms until a light went out suddenly in the hall a few feet from the stairs. Sung paced the hall to her bedroom. He stopped at her room and placed his ear to the paneled door waiting to hear her breathe. Sung quietly listened for a faint sigh before she dosed off to sleep. He stopped his wristwatch at thirty minutes then suddenly fled the house. In a matter of a moment he was back at his car. He picked up a blinking radio receiver.

"Did you time yourself properly this mission?" Nu's voice entered the receiver.

"She lives alone-" He said coldly over his personal radio.

"Good." Nu replied over the receiver with satisfaction.

She continued, "Then the job will be clean."

"Where do I dump the body?" He asked carefully.

"Leave her there." Nu commanded.

"Why?"

"The detective will be too busy searching for her killer then to dig any deeper into my affairs." Nu ended sharply. She knew the detective was becoming savvy about her ties with the underworld and he would soon be a threat. It wouldn't be long before McCall found that Nu Shangxi had a lot to hide.

Chapter 24: Close Call

On the other side of the city....

A few weeks had passed and Eddy was finally let out of the hospital. He didn't limp out of the hospital doors he walked out and the wounds on his legs healed nicely. The doctor's were left mystified over the scientific phenomenon. Oddly enough none of the doctor's gossiped of this strange recovery but the fuzz lingered about the hallways in brief dialogue. Eddy traipsed about the barren city streets like a zombie that freshly rose from the earth. Eddy's thoughts were running over the past tragedy and His old addiction surfacing again. It began pulling Eddy into another fit since he checked into the hospital. He quickly found a nearby phone booth and quickly dialed out. A few rings passed and a tired voice of a man finally came over the receiver.

"H-Hello?" The mysterious voice said.

"Jack?" Eddy answered friendly voice.

"Hey pal," Eddy replied in code over the receiver. "Are you still in the neighborhood?" Jack was hesitant to answer the line and there was a brief silence after the exchange of code.

"Who the heck is this?" Jack snapped over the phone.

"Eddy James," he said.

"We met at The Purple Lady one night, Jack."

"E-Eddy, I remember now but I stopped dealing out there you know the pigs got to me too." He returned over the receiver.

"Switchblade had gotten wrapped up too." Eddy replied.

"Are still messing around with that dancer?" a slight chuckled emerged over the receiver but Eddy ignored his inquiry.

"Not anymore." in a low voice and then a pause came over the receiver.

"Can you meet me at Jackson Heights?"

"You got dough for this, right?"

The dealers question over the receiver while Eddy was counting his cash.

"Yes, same as last deal?"

"You got it. Just be there."

Evening clouds were looming over Eddy and the city was coming into darkness. Among the hour two headlights finally appeared glimmering through the downpour of rain. The rain drops beat down steady on a out dated hatchback and Jack hopped out of the car. Eddy was waiting patiently in the alleyway for him. Jack signaled him to his car. They both traveled back to the car and Jack climbed into his seat. He waited for Eddy to give him the money. Eddy's urge for a high drew his frail body closer to the open window even though he didn't want to part with money. He threw a wad of cash onto the seat and the driver counted the money then finally spoke to him.

"I left the stash by the rubber tree over yonder, just go and pick it up." He whispered to Eddy then slammed his car into drive and finally tore off down the road.

Eddy quickly turned around and noticed a thin tree by a pawnshop. He knelt down slowly and picked up a small brown bag wrapped in a rubber band. Eddy made it to his empty apartment. He shook the rain off his coat and found the couch. There he prepared a new dope needle for injection of heroin. Loneliness was creeping into Eddy's bones and he felt the devil toying with his addiction. It was the climax of another sorrowful moment with Eddy's addiction. His bony fingers pick out the dope from the bag. A mindless pleasure plunged him back into a dream state which made a chaotic world lucid again. He pushed the heroin into his bloodstream. The drug froze him in ecstasy and he began rocking back and forth in a mild fit. The body relaxed back into the seat and finally placed him into a zombie-like state.

Back in Europe...

Across the Atlantic Ocean Nu Shangxi's shipment of porcelain wares were getting loaded onto a commercial liner headed for Europe. Hidden under the bowel of the ship was a load of cocaine and opium which were secretly being smuggled in with porcelain jugs and artifacts as cargo. Nu was ready to flood the underworld markets. She was crafty and had plenty of amnesty to land product around the global cities. Since the Opium King had been collapsed the waters were safe for her pirate drug empire to expand. One of her main contacts were settled just across the borders of Yugoslavia and Romania. She and her body guard arrived at a dated Norman style castle along the country-side. A current deal was being wrapped up for Nu's territories. The main door open and Helzchec appeared standing before them. He was a tall, stocky man with a palsy-ridden face.

Hans Helzchec greeted Nu Shangxi in the candlelight of the vaulted breezeway.

"Good morning, I am sorry I was a little late." He replied looking down at his watch.

"Don't worry, Hans, we all can be a little late sometimes." Nu returned.

His chiseled Romanian features gave her a subtle attraction at first glance but his disfigured frame kept her from a fatal attraction. He was once a Romanian official who lost his position as a result of selling secrets to his countries enemies during a presidential campaign. He now resided on the German border of Budapest completing his plans to dominate the underworld markets with a little help from Yangtze shipping.

"Asander?" Hans continued. "Show our clients in."

Asander was a brawny northerner with a red face and blonde mane. He had been Han's colleague and deadly trained guard. He towered over Nu and her bodyguard, Kazim, like a Norwegian lighthouse. He quickly checked them for any weapons but found nothing of importance.

Chapter 25: Helzchec

"They are clean." Said Asander with assurance after he placed his magnetic gun aside.

"Come." Hans gently directed. Nu and Kazim traveled down a broad hallway decorated in classical limestone arches and local handmade tapestries. They traveled to a spacious medieval ballroom and entered into a private office trimmed in darkened oak wood. The door clanged shut behind like a dungeon gate.

"Sit, comrades." Hans commanded with a Slavic draw. He retreated behind a cherry escritoire. Asander directed them both to velvet-red chairs and finally they sat down.

"Now, about our deal?" He pronounced in malevolence.

"Before you opt out of this deal," she snapped in desperation of the losing proposition.

"I'm listening." He replied.

"You might as well know the Opium King is finished." She declared while staring around the company of anarchists.

"Indeed." Hand returned.

"The time is now to join me with your full cooperation." Said Nu in persuasion. Hans's brow wrinkled with curiosity.

"I heard the delightful news yesterday." Said Hans quietly then turned his eyes directly at Nu.

"Because of his past offenses our deal will soon attract too much attention from international authorities." Hans argued with grief-stricken looks upon his face.

"Not true," replied Nu Shangxi. "With your amnesty and my shipping company we could do much better than him." She answered with a sly grin.

"We shall soon see but now the present shipment coming into Europe is why I am here today?"

"We have a billion delivered to your account when you say the word." A phone rang aloud and Hans quickly picked up.

"See that Nu's shipment of porcelain wares gets safely across the Atlantic without any pests." He continued over the receiver. He carefully whispered back into the receiver then quickly hung up.

"I think we will be able to work well together, miss Shangxi." After Hans gave them a final handshake, Nu and Hazim were safely led back to the airport.

Back in the states...

Mr. Li waited patiently for a call from Eddy. He had been late for his shifts and hadn't paid Mr. Li a visit for many weeks since the hospital. Suddenly Eddy's silhouette suddenly appeared from behind the smoky garage.

"Where have you been?" Asked the Li.

"Around." Eddy replied elusively.

"You're late again for your shift."

Mr. Li was unsatisfied with his answer and he began to search Eddy for any clues about his person. A white hospital tag on Eddy's right hand seized his attention. The anger in Mr. Li's eyes began to subside.

"What is this on your wrist?" Replied Mr. Li.

"It's a hospital tag." Eddy replied.

"Why were you in the hospital?" He looked upon Eddy while holding onto his wrist.

"Nothing, Mr. Li, I was in the hospital for weeks but I'm better now." Eddy replied.

"C'mon Eddy after all these years knowing you, just tell me."

"I was in intensive care for a couple days that's all I remember and I couldn't really call-."

Eddy was on edge over Mr. Li's suspicions. Mr. Li finally dropped his defenses.

"My regrets, I thought you had given up your job!" Mr. Li was still struck with curiosity over Eddy's tardiness. His heavy stares became warm grin and Eddy began to recline a little.

"Okay." Mr. Li replied then placed his tiny hand on Eddy's shoulder like a concerned father.

"Are you alright for work today?" He begged then waited patiently for an answer.

"I think so." Answered Eddy with sincerity in his eyes.

"Good then," Mr. Li replied. "Take a cab around the airport today, okay?" He directed then handed Eddy the keys to the yellow cab.

"The airport?" Eddy returned surprised.

"Just go light today." He Demanded.

Chapter 26: Intruder

"Another cold night without Frank again?" Thought Taylor to her self as she glanced outside at the barren driveway. "He usually calls by now?"

The lights went off and the dark presence of Sung Jinn suddenly arrived. He pulled up to an inconspicuous corner of the street and parked his car. He appeared in all black and ready to bring death. Sung readied his silencer and pushed through the bushes of her house. He entered her house again without making a sound and crept up the stairs. Sung paced slowly down the dark hallway. The hammer of his equalizer was cocked and ready. Her bedroom door was ajar and he waited again like the last mission, waited for her to yawn. Nothing. A rumble emerged behind the door and he was riddled with panic. He pulled a mask over part of his face then fled the other room. The bedroom door flung open and Taylor rolled into the bathroom. Sun Jinn carefully open the closet door and peaked out waiting for Taylor. A flash of headlights from a nearby widow suddenly seized Sung Jinn. He raced to an open window then grappled down the pitched roof of the house. He found a spot under the shade of a falling tree limb and waited there patiently. A loud thud sounded on the roof which sent Taylor into a spin of suspicions. She poked her head out of the window of her room as another thud hit again.

"What could that be at this hour?" She thought to herself as he poked her head out of the bedroom window. A shadow of something seized her attention,

"Who's there?" She shouted out into the cold night. Another thud rang out.

"Damn!" She cried. After another thud she dug through McCall's drawer for a weapon. McCall's 9 mm was left there. She picked up the revolver shaking hands and crept up the attic to check the roof. Another shadow appeared. But this time a shadow kept jumping back and forth by the trees that were hanging alongside of the pitched, shingled roof.

"Whose there?" She called out in a shaken voice.

No sound came from the other side of the roof. Suddenly the slam of a door gripped her with fear. She dashed down the stairs into another room and hid behind the door. A silhouette entered the living room. The shadow of a man slowly began to walk into the dark kitchen. Taylor followed close behind.

"Don't move!"

"Click!"

She shouted into the darkness of the kitchen. The shadowy figure stopped moving and froze in place. Moonlight from the kitchen window revealed back of a man's leather jacket.

"What the heck are you doing in my house?" Taylor screamed in agitation then gripped the handle of her gun with ferocity.

"I-I," said the intruder softly. Taylor still could not make out the face of the intruder.

"Don't even bother." She interrupted.

"Who ever you are, the police will be here any moment!" The lights flicked on suddenly and McCall's face appeared.

"Oh?" Taylor reclined and un-cocked her revolver and swooned at McCall's image standing in the kitchen light.

"Taylor? What are you doing with my gun?" He replied.

"Frank!" She exclaimed. McCall appeared worn out and tired.

"Taylor," he replied. "What's going on?" She finally put down the gun on the counter and threw her arms around McCall.

"I don't know?" She said with a faint cry. "I heard a noise on the roof and I grabbed your revolver."

"It's alright now." He told her.

Sung quietly jumped off the roof and fled by the moonlight. Nu Shangxi would have to wait for her prey to be in her clutches.

Chapter 27: The Meeting with Davis

McCall entered a little late for a meeting with Davis. He limped into his office and stood at attention by his desk.

"Where's my report?" He replied condescendingly.

"Report?" Returned McCall still a little buzzed after the ruckus from the previous night.

"The report on the James shooting?" Replied Davis but McCall was still dazed from the previous night.

"Well, where is it?"

"It's coming along." Said McCall finally snapping too.

"Coming along? You worked on this case for almost two year now.

"This case turned for the worst when we found that kid shot on the floor in Queens, captain, we need more time."

"You started out with tracking down a small time dealer and now its blown up into some more sh*t?" Replied Davis still looking upon the detective scathingly.

"Okay, what I came up with is that shooting may be linked to another triad group that's shipping opium in the states illegally." Said McCall.

"I can't bust 'em until the report is on my desk!" Implied Davis. McCall then eased into a chair with a sigh. Davis remained hovering over McCall with an ill omen stare.

"What's the matter with you this morning anyway, McCall?" Said Davis pacing back and forth like a nervous caged animal.

"What's the matter with me?" Replied McCall disparaged over Davis' charges.

"Yes," said Davis wryly. "That's what I'm asking you? You were late this morning and you look like sh*t!" He exclaimed with disgust.

"Taylor thought someone broke into her house last night." Replied McCall.

"I don't believe you, McCall, not a word!" Davis injected.

McCall rose angrily. "C'mon, Davis, I was up all night for Christ sake!"

"Kid, don't lose your head in all this mess," he responded. "I just want the facts and what I want to know now is the true identity of those triads?"

"I got some leads as to who they are." McCall answered then moved around in his seat nervously trying to get comfortable.

"Really?" Davis remarked folding his arms in apathy over his lackluster plea.

"Then why is there nothing in writing?" Said Davis pacing around his desk.

"I've been busy on the trail of Lou Chang." McCall reported ardently over the negative responses.

"So, what have you found so far?" Pleaded Davis.

"From what I gather the stolen container wound up in some junkies hands, namely Vasquez. Then the shooting took place at Eddy's apartment leaving him nearly dead. And according to Eddy, Vasquez, was seen fleeing after the shooting. When I found the vial I realized Lou Chang had become an instant suspect."

"Any reason why you think so?" Said Davis listening intently to McCall's report. McCall pulled out the ancient vial from his coat. Unwrapped it and placed it on the desk.

"Whoever shot Eddy, may have been after this?" McCall finally reveal one of the pieced of evidence to Davis who was currently gripped over the crystal vial. He picked it up and placed in the light for a better look.

"The vial that I found by the fire escape?" Said McCall while Davis swished the liquid back and forth in the light.

"The junkies call it by the street name, red-nine, forensics' lab mention it was a rare opiate." Responded McCall.

"Who did they get this from?"

"I think Nu Shangxi is shipping more than just porcelain wares overseas?"

"You think so, Sherlock?" Replied Davis smugly.

"Strange?" Remarked Davis. "Chinese language characters?" Davis inspected the script upon the face of the ancient vial.

"Sounds like you finally maybe onto something here." He said.

"I read the article last week." Davis remarked.

"If we don't stop this drug operation from hitting the streets there will be hell to pay."

"I'm trying my best, captain!"

"Get some kind of report together on what's been going on and get some rest." With his last command McCall finally marched out of the office.

Chapter 28: Taylor's House

The night sky began to settle over McCall's apartment in Queens as he turned down the main street. He noticed a parked car in front of the apartment building. McCall hopped out of his car and prepared his 9mm. McCall had been on edge since the last break in and didn't want to take any more chances. He crept with his back to the wall and slowly paced up the stairs. The hallway light had been off for weeks and the hallways were still dark. Only the tactical rail light from his compact lit the way.

"Another break in?" McCall thought to himself as he finally reached the top flight of stairs.

Suddenly a door slammed shut down the hall and a tall silhouette followed behind.

"It was the stalker that was lurking around Lou Chang's apartment from before." Thought McCall as he chased after his shadow down the hall.

"He finally found where I lived?" Thought McCall traveling down the fire escape.

But it was too late for McCall and the nightly intruder had gotten away once again. McCall rushed to search his apartment.

"Damn!" Said McCall while he kept tripping over the trash in the apartment.

He grew nervous after witnessing piles of fallen books and over turned chairs. The floor was swimming in papers and clothes. Some files were also strewn across the kitchen. A pile of pictures suddenly seized McCall's attention.

"Taylor!" He cried aloud when he found his lovers pictures fanned out on the floor with other documents. He knew they were spread out in the open for a darker purpose.

Whoever it was they had been tracking McCall down for some time and Taylor might be next. McCall rushed to his hidden gun locker in the closet and armed himself with a twelve-gauge and a hefty sum of rounds. He raced to his car and sped off towards Taylor's house.

After he hit some speed traps outside of his county a team of police cars chased close behind with sirens roaring but McCall remained concentrated and didn't bother to look behind. He finally arrived at Taylor's house. He jumped out with his shotgun in hand ignoring the police warnings. They instinctively marched behind him with guns blazing.

"He's here now?" McCall whispered to himself.

The same car that was parked in his lot from the previous encounter was now parked in the front of her house. The front door was busted open and McCall felt faint as he took another step closer to the scene.

"Taylor!" He called out her name again while remaining pressed against the brick wall for cover. Nothing sounded. He took another step in. It appeared the stalker hit her house too but this time blood stained the walls of the living room and the carpets even the chandeliers had blood on them.

"Damn!" McCall knew what happened to her and he was too late.

A dim light overhead shown Taylor's dead body was laid to waist in a pile of gore on the kitchen floor. The kitchen room was turned into a nightmare with walls dripping in blood spatter. He knelt down and pressed his tired body against hers.

"Did you hear that?" A thud atop the second story alarmed McCall. He nervously reached for his shotgun in a fit of vengeance. He jumped to his heels and made a run for the second floor.

"He's here." McCall shouted. "I know it."

The other officers finally caught up to McCall and ended their chase at Taylor's front door. Police radio out on his CB.

"Officer Johnson here, we got to break in, possible homicide, 38th and North."

"Look at this mess, Johnson!" Cried the first officer upon entering the bloody house. The police caught McCall pacing the floors for the murderer. They quickly placed their aim upon the unruly detective.

"Drop your weapon!" Replied the nervy cop. He kept his revolver pegged at McCall's back. But McCall didn't turn around to meet them instead he kept moving towards his target.

"Frank McCall? Detective, Frank McCall?" The earnest voice of the county sergeant called out to the detective. The sergeant recognized the name over the CB description coming over the station radio. McCall was known around the precincts as a tough detective with a no nonsense game-play.

"Put it away, Johnson, its Detective McCall from the New York City precinct, he must be undercover here?"

"Detective McCall?" Johnson said in a fit of doubt then looked upon his partner with indignation.

"From narcotics?" The Sergeant explained.

"Still doesn't ring a bell." Replied Johnson still embodied with suspicion. Then McCall appeared again in the blood stained hallways.

"He's still here!" McCall shouted. Johnson finally put his gun away. Insanity was welling in his eyes as he carefully studied Taylor's dripping blood upon the wall.

"Who are you looking for, McCall?" Asked the sergeant.

"There's no time, Sergeant." said McCall finally dashing up the hallway steps in the search for the mysterious intruder. He ascended to the top floor and the bedrooms were hauntingly silent. McCall carefully tiptoed through the dark rooms peeking into each of them leading with the barrel of his shotgun. The police hurried up to the stairs after McCall.

"No one's here, McCall." Replied the Sergeant. He said flashing their flashlight in the darkness of the rooms.

"But this guy is sneaky, Sergeant." He remarked with eyes peeping from out of the shadows. "He had my girlfriend's photos out on the floor as if he was planning something."

"That's a common code for killers, eh?"

"I've been on this case for months." Remarked McCall.

McCall crept closer to the bathroom stall. It was dark and nothing was there. McCall turned around slowly. Suddenly a closet door began to inch open.

"McCall," cried the Sergeant. "Watch out!"

A light flashed across Sung Jinn's head which was peaked out of the closet.

"Bang!" A bullet ejected out of Sung Jinn's gun.

McCall slipped the bullet aimed for his head then spun a roundhouse kick. It loosened the silencer out of the deadly assassin's hand but the pressure in McCall was building up over his dead girlfriend and he didn't think twice at the thought of revenge.

"Tonight you die!" Said McCall with an ill-faded grin then finally pulled the trigger.

"*Kachoom!*" Sounded the shotgun. The blast splayed Sun Jinn's face all over the hallway. New blood-spatter decorated Taylor's walls with crimson red.

"Damn, McCall, You could have just detained the SOB!" Said Johnson sarcastically.

"He had to pay for the mess down stairs, Johnson." McCall grimly replied. McCall hovered over the dead body then began to rifle through his jackets and slacks. There was nothing on his persons except a strange I.D. card from Canada. Sung Jinn's Asian features matched the card to perfection. An air of curiosity around his alias.

"What do you make on him, McCall?" Asked the Sergeant.

"I don't know? He could be linked to a triad that I am investigating." He replied. "I will get some answers!"

Meanwhile across the globe...

Nu Shangxi's shipment was being delivered to foreign shores. A ten-ton vessel landed safely in Bordeaux, France. The guards never suspected the big shipment of porcelain wares to be a safeguard for the dark deal and Han's trucks safely arrived at the ports.

"The shipments have gone through, Miss Shangxi." Said her dark associate over the private phone.

"Good." She replied coldly. "Make sure Hans gets my regards for the favor, good day." She remarked then hung up the phone.

Han's crew had no trouble taking the shipment from France to German borders. It seemed as though Nu Shangxi and Hans Helzchec seemed to hit it off as sinister partners in a dark deal when the last truck crossed German borders. The shipment of drugs would soon hit Europe's underworld.

Chapter 29: Calling It Quits

McCall had to quit the case after Taylor had been murdered. Aside from the countless clues and the endless searches for suspects, McCall, had to leave his badge on the desk. Davis entered his office while he was packing his things.

"I'm sorry, McCall, its still a negative on the identity of her killer." Davis came with the bad news.

"I knew this day would come," he said grimly.

"These things happen to cops everyday." Davis implied.

"The case got personal and she always warned me that it would end like this." McCall said sobbing.

"Well, your still a hero in my book." Davis said then placed his huge hand on McCall s shoulder.

"What's going to happen to the case?" Asked McCall.

"I don't know but this may go to the file as unsolved?" He explained. Davis opened a file with some photos.

"Aside the suspect that killed Taylor we have Chang, Vasquez, Nu Shangxi, and Fists are all wrapped up in this case. We can't handle this even with you on the team."

"I still don't believe that her killer was from Canada, do you?" McCall replied.

"No, we figured that Eddy James was involved with something bigger." Said Davis then McCall began placing some picture frames in a box.

"Captain, there was more to this whole thing then I once thought." He continued. "I realized when I let Vasquez go after an interrogation."

"We will still be searching the city for Vasquez and his drug operation." Warned Davis.

"I let him go after I took him in one night after a bar fight.

"Don't worry, McCall, some of our best guys are on it."

"Chang got away that night as well." McCall said. "He was there to get the drugs off of Vasquez but he left empty handed.

"Well, they are both still in the city and they'll turn up either dead or alive." Davis returned aiming confidence at McCall.

"What about Nu Shangxi?" McCall asked.

"The Shangxi case has been handed over to the Feds for further investigation and she will be watched accordingly." He said.

"Well, that leaves Eddy James."

"Eddy James will have to keep an eye on him and keep him off the streets but I have a feeling his killers will be back." Davis replied.

"Don't you think it's strange that he hasn't died yet?"

"What do you mean, McCall?"

"It must be the drug?"

"You mean the drug he took from the vial?" Davis gave McCall a wry look. "You don't really believe all that old Taoist folklore, do you?" Davis snapped at McCall shaking his senses.

"No, but the myth has past my mind quite frequently."

"The test on the liquid only came up opium." Laughed Davis.

"I feel there's more to the drug that may end the case." Implied McCall.

"Don't fool yourself, detective, we got this whole case under control."

"But, Davis, he took over a hundred bullets and didn't die!" Explained McCall.

"It's nothing new, McCall, there were a ton of incidents of druggies surviving bullets and they mostly were found on PCP."

"But Eddy James incident was surely different, don't you agree?" Said McCall.

"He's just a drug addict, detective, it shouldn't concern you anymore your off this case and you decided to leave the force."

"I know, captain, I am calling it quits."

"I got to go, I'll see you round, McCall." Davis said then finally left the office.

Chapter 30: The Fists

Eddy was still on route hustling pedestrians when a past thoughts emerged through his psyche. It didn't matter that he had been shot twice or beaten to death by Switchblade. He didn't even care that his best friend betrayed him but all the years of not knowing who his parents were he still knew who he was.

Twenty years ago…

A storm was surfacing in the winds over a vacant concrete lot. The sky was gray from storm clouds that were forming on the horizon. Eddy and Vasquez approached the concrete pit as teenagers. They carefully walked past a bum wrestling with a city newspaper under the highway overpass and prepared for another street fight with the Fists. The hollow lot was a hangout for the local hoods in the city and it had been baptized by blood and haunted by ghostly cries from previous gang wars. The whole area was deemed too dangerous at night even for the local authorities and wandering pedestrian wouldn't dare cross it alone. The local gangs used to call it, hell's pit. Loud cries were echoing with the clamor of new misfits. Eddy and Vasquez watched from the shadows of the overpass as the hoods of mixed races formed opposite sides down below.

"How many kids do you think are down there?" Vasquez asked gazing upon the crowd.

"At least a hundred." Eddy returned and a smirk fell from Vasquez's face. A loud thunderclap emerged from the sky. Eddy drew a sense of liberation from the thunder in the clouds that day and he recalled why he became a Dragon. That day the gangs were banded together again ready to die for another useless cause. They all wanted to profit from Chinatown's corners. The corners became the main profit for pimping and drugs over the years and The Fists and the Dragons had been planning to take it over since the late eighties. The streets were wild during Eddy's youth and there were no rules except surviving the dangerous nights. The Dragons could no longer run from the Fists after they took over the local street corners and they were getting stronger as a territorial threat. This final battle was to end it all.

Among the jittery crowd another thunderclap emerge out of the abyss of the sky and it was clear now that the "gods of war" approved. The Fists came prepared armed heavily with knives and bats. A deathly look came upon Vasquez's face for a moment as the Dragon's piled into the concrete hollow in great numbers to meet the Fists.

"I don't know if we're going to make it alive this time?" Said Vasquez faintly as he flicked open the blade of his stiletto.

"You know what happened to Johnny?" Said Vasquez huffing a bit over his dead teenage friend. Eddy nodded slightly with fear running across his brow. And his face seemed to turn pale as he kept a heavy stare upon the crowd down below.

"Y-you know he didn't survive the last fight?" Then Eddy grew silent and he stared upon his friend with great intensity.

"Let's make this fight the one they never forget." Eddy returned coolly as his grip tightened on his chipped bat. Sweat perspired from his brow as the anticipation of the big fight was drawing close and he knew it was the point of no return. Cries from the large crowd suddenly calmed like that before a rainstorm and Eddy's heart began to race. Then a crack of lighting lit up the sky and another scream emerged out of the

silence of the moment. Again the sky shook with thunder and the battle began. More than a hundred hoods and thugs clashed together in a bloody encounter. The swing of Eddy's bat cracked through a horde of unsuspecting Fist's. The force of Eddy's bat pushed through the rain, crushing a few skulls and instantly spilling fresh blood across the lot. A rogue punch cut through the blood feud and knocked Eddy back to the concrete.

Vasquez however fought aside Eddy for his life beside him armed with a stiletto blade. Amid the struggle he slashed a trail through venomous attacks with his blade. Eddy rose to his feet shaking off the last punch all the while Vasquez's thin blade cut through flesh of the infidel. Rain and blood poured forth from the sky until another bolt of lightning from the gods struck. It carried across the sky and landed over a squad car. The cops jumped from their squad cars and into the danger zone. They opened the crowd of teen gang banger with charged shotguns firing into the onslaught. The horde of hoods scattered like an army of ants. Eddy however was quick to leave hell's pit alive. He left without Vasquez and vanished into the night. He avoided capture by ducking in and out of alleys like a desperado that just escaped the hangmen. Eddy finally found refuge at a nearby abandon apartment building. He tripped up the crumbling steps and stopped at the main entrance of the building. He winced at the fowl stench of a bum covered with booze.

"Crash!" Eddy kicked an empty bottle across the floor.

"They'll never find me here." He said to himself as his worn sneaker made the first attempt at kicking in a random door. Eddy brushed by the broken glass and arrived at a boarded enclosure. The outdated twenties artdeco arch way was covered with wood planks The brick walls were grayed from time and the window broken by previous convicts hiding from the police.

The night was silent and only the autumnal wind seemed to be present. Eddy sat back quietly and listened to the police siren cutting through the silence of the night like a razor. His doubts about lying low in the abandon apartment building were soon over when he pushed open a door with faded paint. He crept slowly into the dark apartment panting all the while proceeding with caution. The roaring sirens made him shutter a bit as they passed up and down the streets but Eddy kept pacing the dark hall of the abandon building. He tripped over some empty bottles & trash looking for a place to rest. Eddy was a bit nervous from the ghostly whispers of a vagrant whaling in the building. He walked further down the dark hallway filled with refuse and dead rats. He began to feel its emptiness until a strange green light drew him into another vacant room. Eddy walked even further into the room. But the room was pitched dark and he began feeling in the darkness for stability. He padded his hands over a mysterious black bag then drew his hands back in fear. Another wino appeared dead basking in reflection of the green traffic lights. Eddy noticed he had been shot that night and dumped there. The bum was still frozen dead in time like an old relic. He had some blood on his white shirt but death didn't bother Eddy much. He waved his hands before the bum but he didn't make a move. Eddy decided to leave the room and continued through the hall in search for rest. A room without a door caught Eddy and entered. A light flickered in the distance. The fears of that night began to subside as Eddy settled down in a pile of old rags. The light gleaming from the bar across the way entertained him while trying to fall asleep.

Chapter 21: The Abandoned

Eddy sighed with regret at the sight of rubbish around him. "Could this be my only future?" Asked Eddy to himself while pushing aside some of the debris in the room. He finally found a pathway leading deeper into the hall. Glowing eyes appeared. An alley cat was luring him into another small room. Only a few rays of moonlight poked through the splintered windowpane. It was there, in that deserted room he finally felt at ease. Tired of running and tired of hiding. Eddy slid his back down slowly against the crumbling drywall until he fell into a comfortable stupor. Loneliness now began to engulf him.

The streets no longer echoed with police sirens. Eddy was curious to see why. He then peeped through the windowpane. Only the bums and prostitutes creeping along the sidewalks were present. He watched them carefully in silence until their shadows began to fade between the street lights and emptied into the darkness of the night. The scene was all too familiar to him as a teen living on the streets. After the night passed along he remembered lonelier nights gazing aimlessly out of the broken window pane of his orphanage. The moon seemed to be the only friend around and he basked in its light as the familiar comfort he once knew.

Morning light finally broke through the window and into the room and only a few crawling roaches were present to greet him.

"Bang!" A lot percussion rang out into the sky.

Eddy jumped at the sound of gunfire and poked his head out of the window. He looked down from the window and realized that he was nearly thirty stories to the top.

"Hey, you up there?" Shouted one of the on duty police. Eddy ducked low after discovering a group of squad cars surrounding the building. His heart began to race with fear. He paced the room in panic then he glance out of the window. Eddy dashed out of the room then down the top floor fire-escape. In descending from floor to floor he wondered how he had gotten into this mess before hand. His doubts were coming true that morning as the cops began to opened fire at him while descending the fire escape. Eddy finally made it down then hid among broken-down cars in the lot. The team of cops scattered around the lot searching for his whereabouts while he kept rolling under different cars for cover. He waited in heavy breath embracing another bout of bad fortune.

"Give up! You're surrounded!" Called one of the officers. The front entrance of the gray building was swarming in blue uniforms. The door swung open and one of the winos from the previous night strutted out of the dilapidated building. His hands were raised and he quickly fell prey to the crowd of authorities. Eddy had a clean getaway and remained in the shadows of the dark hallways of the building until sunset.

Chapter 32: Territories

Eddy had remembered that he survived a deadly encounter with the Fists once before. He was run ragged from the previous night's interlude and the stench of blood and sweat reminded him that still needed a shower. He scoured the local neighborhoods looking for some rest. He thought of a run-down pizzeria on the edge of town and it was the first place in his sights for a rest. He was a little winded when he entered the shop but he managed to get the doors open. Eddy entered with an ill faded grin upon his face and the shopkeeper could see the grief from the previous night worn on his expressions.

"Hey," Shouted the pizzeria's shopkeeper. "Where you been, kid?" He asked flinging fries into the fryer. Eddy found a stool and began to place heavy stares upon the shopkeeper.

"I've been around." Eddy returned quietly.

"Is that all you can say?" The shopkeeper replied poking for more information from Eddy.

"Like I said, around." Eddy replied.

"One of your buddies were looking for you." Said the shopkeeper jarringly.

"Oh Really?" Asked Eddy. The shopkeeper dropped the pizza dough then look upon Eddy with suspicion.

"He had bunch' a hoods around him and said his name was Chico." Eddy's eyes seemed to pop out of his thin teenage skull. He felt like he knew that name.

"He said that you two have to settle."

"Great," Eddy returned cynically.

"So, what'll it be today, kid?"

"Soda with ice."

"Say, have you been around city square lately?"

"No," said Eddy dipping low into his seat. "Why do ask?" He remarked.

"I thought I saw you with a bunch of kids running from the cops the other night?" He remarked with curiosity raising upon his brows. The shopkeeper held a steady hand over-filled cup of soda and placed it before Eddy. Eddy suddenly jumped to his feet in frustration and prepared to leave.

"It wasn't me, I swear!" A look of despair turned Eddy's face pale with fright. He dropped the soda from his hand and booked down the narrow entrance and finally ducked out of the pizzeria before the shopkeeper could grab him.

"Hey!" Before the shopkeeper could reach Eddy he was gone. Eddy didn't stop walking until he reached the corner of a depressed neighborhood. He turned on the street and walked hastily down the broken sidewalks. The buildings were blackened with construction debris stuck of animal and human urine. Eddy traveled down the street and entered a narrow alley. He knew word got around fast in the city and he could be nailed to gossip. He kicked away some dogs and cats picking through trash then followed the steps of a row house that was still standing among the rest of the destroyed buildings. There he stopped before a rotted piece of plywood. He knocked twice upon the door with number six spray painted on it. The boarded entrance immediately opened. A skinhead appeared smoking a joint. He was doused with grit, stains and tribal tattoos. His teeth gleamed with a hue of green stain and his skin was paled

with yellow. Smoke emanated from his nostrils and Eddy's eyes began to tear.

"Grandpa at the pizza shop knows I wasn't pinched by the cops last night." Said Eddy panting.

"Get in here!" Barked the skinhead. Eddy seemed to balk at his command and Eddy looked upon the junkie with a childish curiosity. Finally his eyes captured a patrol car in the distance and a sudden fright pushed Eddy into the crack house.

*"I said move it!" Barked the skinhead. Eddy jumped into the mysterious house and closed the boarded door. A tall man hovered behind him. *His features were hidden under the shadows of the dimly lit room.*

"Hey, Switchblade?" Barked the skinhead. A dangerous looking man's chiseled features poked into the light.

"Did we get the new stuff?" Switchblade turned to the skinhead.

"Who's the new guy?"

"Don't worry about him, Mickey." Returned the skinhead.

"We don't get the stuff until it reaches our shores." Replied Switchblade turning to Eddy who now was attentive through the conversation.

"I'd have my eyes on the Fist's." Warned the skinhead.

"What about them?" Switchblade replied with a zest for curiosity.

"They have an eye on us all the time."

"The boys are well prepared." Switchblade answered back.

"If all goes well the pay is well worth the wait." Switchblade caught Eddy staring too deeply at him. He threw a menacing look upon Eddy.

"What are you looking at, kid?" He pulled out a Switchblade blade and held it close to Eddy.

"You know why they used to call me Switchblade in prison?" Eddy said nothing then Switchblade pulled his blade away.

Chapter 33: Mr. Li

The Dragons were a young triad wanting a name and the cops recognized them as a threat to city life. Eddy had been with them as a gang member for three years since he left his school. Although being a Dragons member seemed to fill the void in his life there was only one positive force that seemed to hold Eddy together. Mr. Li was a much different man, a secure man, who played a strong role in Eddy's young adult life. Mr. Li was an elderly Asian man with wisdom pouring out from the demeanor in his face. His posture was always cast in a droop and his mandarin lips curled around and frozen in place like that of a wise old dragon. He represented wisdom to Eddy and the middle-age sage commanded respect. He was as an exemplary figure through the years of his adolescence. Eddy's first encounter with Mr. Li when while he was meditating outside on his porch on along the main street.

"Hey, Mister what are you doing there?" Asked Eddy. Mr. Li did not answer Eddy and he remained quiet.

"Hey mister, do you know what time it is?" Asked Eddy. Mr. Li still remained quiet and meditating. Eddy then turned away annoyed by the wait.

"It's six o'clock." Mr. Li finally answered.

"Say, mister, what is it that were you doing there?"

"Meditating." Li snapped at the curious teenager.

"What is that?" Eddy returned with a childishly-like remark.

"Meditating? It helps with inner pain." Li said again.

"What did you say your name was?"

"Paul Li." He replied.

"Li? What kind of name is that?"

"Chinese."

"I had a friend of mine who was Chinese but he was deported."

"So sorry for him?"

"What is your name young one?"

"Eddy James." He replied.

"Well, it must be dinner time for you Eddy. You must be leaving for home now."

"I don't have a home or a place to eat."

"Come eat with me for the night then."

At that moment Mr. Li had Eddy grew together in a relationship that would last until his adulthood. Li knew the path of Eddy's life was dark but the world around him was even darker. Mr. Li secretly knew the underworld was winning over Eddy's soul with each passing year and there wasn't much he could say. Only Eddy himself could end such a war inside him. One night the rain came upon the city and would not stop. Mr. Li was just closing up the taxi garage when Eddy walked out with a gun in his hand.

"What's the problem, Eddy are you in trouble?" Li asked with curiosity.

"Nothing, man, j-just don't asked me tonight, okay?" Eddy returned with trouble in his eyes ignoring Li.

"Here, Eddy, pay day." Mr. Li handed him his pay. Eddy snatched the check from him and hopped back into his car. The garage doors slammed shut behind Mr. Li. Then Eddy and Vasquez sped off in their car. Late that night Mr. Li awoke at

the sound of guns shots that rang out in the night. The alarms went off at a local bank where Eddy and Vasquez appeared fleeing and drenched with blood.

"We need to find cover quick!" Eddy Cried cruising away in their car. Eddy turned the corner of Li's neighborhood. He knocked upon the door and Mr. Li finally answered.

"Eddy? Why are you here at this late hour?" Mr. Li asked.

"I-I need a place for the night, Mr. Li." Eddy appeared to Mr. Li with the same troubled look on he had before.

"What's the problem, son?"

"I can't talk now!" He barked at Li. The porch light revealed the sight of blood that pushed Mr. Li away from the Eddy by the door.

"Are you hurt?" Asked Li.

"Please, you got to let me in!" Eddy cried by the partly open door. Li finally allowed Eddy through the door.

The next day...

Eddy was silent and Mr. Li did not talk much for the remainder of the day. Eddy grew insecure every time the noise of a siren passed down the city streets. Mr. Li could tell from the sickly look in his eyes that Eddy was dealing with a dark moment in his life.

"So, Eddy what happened to you the other night?" Li asked then placed a great concerned look upon Eddy. He withdrew from Li's inquiry and just shrugged.

"I-I just don't have the time to talk about it today, Mr Li." Eddy snapped. Li grabbed Eddy's arm with firmness.

"I need to know if you hurt anyone last night." Li replied.

"I have nothing to say about last night." Eddy returned while wiggling out of Li's grip. Eddy began to walk away from Mr. Li slowly and finally he turned around to face him. Eddy broke down in front of Li and finally confessed.

"I shot a man last night but he didn't die." Eddy said. Mr. Li's head dropped with shame.

"Why would you do such a thing?" Li returned.

"I-I don't know."

"Did your friend lead you to do this thing?"

"N-no." Said Eddy quivering before Li. Li could sense Vasquez's shadow which seemed to lurk behind Eddy confession.

"I had to Mr. Li," said Eddy. "I needed the money."

"But you have a job here and I even gave you an apartment!" Li shouted.

"You just don't understand, Mr. Li."

"What don't I understand?" Li asked in desperation.

"I told you it shouldn't concern you anymore!"

"But it does, Eddy, if you broke the law!" Cried out Li.

"I suggest you tell no one, it may save your life." Eddy said threateningly.

"You are a fool for your friend, Eddy." Li growled at Eddy. Mr. Li walked away and Eddy stood by sighing. His life was torn apart at the seams and after the fight with Li things weren't the same.

Chapter 34: Bloody Fist

Presently...

DAWN WAS SETTING IN OVER the city and Eddy was turning in for the night. The streets have cooled down from the crime waves now that Switchblade was imprisoned and The Opium King was apprehended but Vasquez was still running from the triad with the box in his possession. Although the street seemed to be safer than before the there was something else hiding in the shadows of the city. The moon's light was devoid of a true destiny that was now lurking for Eddy James. The dimness of Eddy's apartment was filling up with the glowing TV set and the moans of a skin flick. Eddy was finally getting comfortable for the night when a knock came upon the door.

"Just a minute!" Shouted Eddy.

He dug through the couch pillows and pulled out his revolver. He crept with poise to the front door with gun cocked & loaded.

"Who's there?"

"I said whose there?" Another knock came upon the door with no answer.

Nothing again. A moment of silence came by and then a crash came through the apartment window by the fire escape. Eddy shot into the void of the apartment but missed the shadowy figure that kept disappearing in and out of the moonlit darkness.

"I'll shoot!" He screamed again and again. The shadowy figure came across Eddy with a slash from a large blade. Eddy dodged the razor sharp edge again as it slashed through the darkness in the room.

"Bang!" A blast rang out from Eddy's revolver.

Eddy shot a round of lead but missed. He made a run for the light switch by the main wall of the room. Eddy quickly realized that another triad gang member had broken into the apartment. But this He knew it was time to finish the job. Eddy's nerves began to grow tense as he steadied his trigger finger on the gun in hopes to blast away the prowler. He found some confidence and took a shot. It ricocheted off the white-bricked wall of the room. Suddenly Eddy's last moments came to an end when a sharp spike of a knife came down from behind him on his skull. This time the knife came swiftly with a mortal blow. Blood trickled down Eddy's face and more blood poured out onto the floor.

The triad danced around his dying victim like a proud warrior. Eddy was now helpless as he lay dying. He slowly faded into a coma from head trauma. Eddy coughed some blood up on the floor. Then a silence of darkness came upon Eddy. His poor life choices seemed to finally catch up with him that night and he took it like a rain check that was past due. It wasn't just the triad that snagged Eddy's life short it was the whole gambit which finally crushed him. Visions of those in his past life began to flash, Mr. Li, Vasquez, even a night with Pandora flashed before his dying brain. The young triad struck his finger in Eddy's blood and drew a closed fist on the white-bricked walls then plucked out his blade out of Eddy's skull. He fled from the open window into the night never to be known as Eddy's slayer. It wasn't long before the cops were called and flooded the scene of the crime. McCall rushed to the hospital after he got wind of Eddy's attack. A couple of hours passed and a doctor finally came out into the waiting room.

"I'm sorry to tell you that he might be comatose for life." Said the surgeon. "A knife wound punctured through his cerebellum and damaged most of his central nervous system and it just shut down on him but he didn't die."

"I see, doctor." McCall's eyes dropped low at the news.

"Do you need the copy of the medical briefing, detective?"

"No, I am not handling this case any longer."

"Good night, detective." McCall finally walked out of the hospital and out of the case for good.

Chapter 35: The Sanitarium

The last day in court..

The courts practically threw the book at Eddy James's criminal record and he was given no endowments for his condition by the judge. The detectives wrapped up the case as an unsolved gang incident and Eddy was left to the devices of the state sanitarium. There wasn't much Eddy could do while in a coma with brain damage. All he could do was cling to a shoddy life-support system and wait for the visits from the medical staff. You could still see the half-ass stitch work on his scalp from the inner city clinic. It was amazing to see that anyone really care for Eddy or his situation. The door of his room opened suddenly and Detective McCall entered then began to watch over Eddy.

"Eddy, can you hear me?" McCall begged while Eddy remained a drooling mess.

"I tried to fight them on this but I couldn't win this time-" McCall cried with enraged emotions. Nothing else was left of Eddy James life but tragedy. McCall even sank in off duty hours for this case only to wind up with a murdered girlfriend and a bigger puzzle with mismatched pieces that didn't to fit all together. There wasn't enough evidence that he could find but he never gave up his theories. McCall was the guy that helped bring down the Opium King and even tied up the notorious Switchblade. If the city knew any such a hero it was McCall even though the crimes committed by the underworld were countless in number.

The door closed behind him and McCall left Eddy for good this time. There was nothing left for him to figure out. McCall did his job and risked enough of his life for this case. He wanted off of this case and wanted a new job. There wasn't much more he could do about the cities troubles. Meanwhile a new power was emerging from the underworld. Nu Shangxi secretly took over the rest of the Opium King's unknown territories and drug operations. Nu, however, was still kept searching the lost artifact in the city. Time finally stopped for Eddy James and life didn't seem real after the attempted murder.

A darker path kept Eddy from living an good life and there were many souls like him. Death was now knocking on his door and the end seem to keep creeping up on him with every last breath. The priest he once knew came into visit and made an absolution while Eddy was still breathing in his coma. Mr. Li entered one last time and meditated with Eddy. The meditation was quiet and a relaxing silence was in the room. Suddenly the heart monitor began to beep. Mr. Li called a nurse and she readily prepared Eddy but Eddy's monitor stopped beeping when his heart gave out. However the poisonous tsung-di was still lingering within his soul and body.

After Death...

The ancient drug was made by Chao Huang to preserve spirit and body while in the midst of death. Since Eddy's former life was filled with grimness and his spiritual life after was still filled with the same grief. He became like a ghost with unfinished business. There was no hope in hell for his soul nor was there any sense on earth for a dark spirit like him. There was no human-response left in his hospital room. Eddy's been fighting for his identity his life but there were no doors of opportunity just dark streets and darker friends. Fate now had handed him his final card and there wasn't anyone around who could help him now. Consequently, Eddy's consciousness awoke again and flash of light reveals a human heart still beating outside of his chest...

Chapter 36: Eternal

Out West...

A HOSPITAL JUST OUTSIDE OF Wichita, John Smithton was recouping after another tragic heart surgery. Martha Smithton was sitting outside the surgery room watching the clock and waiting patiently for the final word on John. Finally a doctor approached Martha with alarm then her eyes grew dim.

"Excuse, me, are you Martha Smithton?" He asked with calmness but Martha was on edge.

"Why, yes, what seems to be the problem?" She returned.

"After the surgery on your husband, John," the doctor suddenly fell into silence and a look of remorse suddenly came upon his face.

"I am afraid we found that more organs were damaged in the crash."

"Oh, dear what will I do?" Martha cried.

"The medical team has already sent out to hunt for an organ donor."

"Why does this have to happened to us?" She cried. The doctor looked to console her.

"We have found a donor and he will be better in a few years' time." Although death seemed to be knocking upon the Smithton's door there was grim chance that her husband may survive the tragic event.

A few months later...

The city coroner investigated Eddy's anatomy strictness if his eye and all the medical test prevail that his organs were in health after the heart had been removed for transplantation. Another man walked into the morgue with a file in hand.

"Here's the rest of the James file for the Smithton transplant," he said. "This seems pretty interesting report."

"His body had been through several gunshot wounds before his death but there was not a scratch on his anatomy?"

"They used heart anyway?" The assistant asked with amazement.

"They were a desperate, you know how it is." The coroner returned.

"Wouldn't you do the same if you needed an organ? Besides the heart was still in decent condition." The assistant replied.

"I guess?" Said the coroner while doping up a needle.

"Did you happen to read anything more on him?" Asked the assistant.

"I have not read all the facts yet." Returned the coroner.

"He went in the hospital and the medical team at the St. Vincent New York clinic found some foreign drug in his blood."

"What else do you know?"

"Some type of strange opiate or it could've been mix up with phencyclidine or type of hallucinogens like LSD." Implied the assistant.

"Hmmm?" The corner hummed with interest.

"Well, this is the file." Said the assistant.

“I’ll look through it later.” Replied the coroner. “Here, take some shots of these tattoos will you?”

Meanwhile Back at the Hospital...

Bloody aprons and machines were clicking in a room. John Smithton was now sleeping in his hospital room with life support. John was finally recouping hours after his transplant surgery.

To be continued...